Also by Dyan Sheldon

Harry and Chicken

Harry the Explorer

Harry on Vacation

My Brother Is a Visitor from Another Planet

MY BROTHER IS A SUPERHERO

Dyan Sheldon

illustrated by Derek Brazell

CANDLEWICK PRESS
CAMBRIDGE, MASSACHUSETTS

Text copyright © 1994 by Dyan Sheldon
Illustrations copyright © 1994 by Derek Brazell

First U.S. edition 1996

Library of Congress Cataloging-in-Publication Data

Sheldon, Dyan.
My brother is a superhero / Dyan Sheldon ;
illustrated by Derek Brazell. — 1st U.S. ed.
Sequel to: My brother is a visitor from another planet.
Summary: When confronted by bullies, nine-year-old Adam
wishes he could ask his older brother for help but is
not sure that Keith will come through for him.
ISBN 1-56402-624-8
[1. Brothers — Fiction. 2. Sibling rivalry — Fiction.
3. Bullies — Fiction.] I. Brazell, Derek, ill. II. Title.
PZ7.S54144Mv   1996
[Fic] — dc20   95-33665

10 9 8 7 6 5 4 3 2 1

Printed in the United States

This book was typeset in Berkeley Oldstyle.

Candlewick Press
2067 Massachusetts Avenue
Cambridge, Massachusetts 02140

For Tom and Dan

Chapter One

The score was two all and the crowd was on its feet. My knee was bleeding and it had started to rain, but I didn't care. All I could think of was the game. There was less than a minute left to play.

Babidge got the ball from Anuli. Anuli passed it to King. King, cornered, spun around and kicked fiercely. It was a desperate move, but a lucky one. The ball sailed clear across the field to where Andrews stood waiting—all alone. The crowd went crazy. Andrews raced toward the goal like a lizard. A lizard with really good foot coordination. I was all alone, too, but on the west side. I started running toward Andrews.

"*An-*drews! *An-*drews! *An-*drews! *An-*drews!"

Faster and faster. Time ticked away.

The crowd was beside itself with tension and excitement.

"*An-*drews! *An-*drews! *An-*drews! *An-*drews!"

And then Cross and Bui came out of nowhere. Foaming at the mouth, Cross closed in from the right. Bui bore down from the left in a mist of mud, his eyes wild.

"*An-*drews! *An-*drews! *An-*drews!"

Andrews looked around in panic. He was feet from the goal, but he was stranded between Cross, Bui, and Hogan, the goalie. He didn't have a hope, and he knew it.

The commentator was counting the seconds. 10 . . . 9 . . . 8 . . .

A ripple ran through the stadium. It was a miracle! Another player had appeared behind Bui.

The crowd changed its chant. "*Wig*-gins! *Wig*-gins! *Wig*-gins!" it roared.

I'd been waiting all season for this chance. The chance to be a hero. The chance to score the winning goal. Like a bullet in a striped jersey and muddy boots, I streaked past Bui, cutting between him and Andrews. My blood thundered. My heart raced. My training and patience were about to pay off. My moment had come at last! There was the goal post. There was the goalie. There was the opening. I aimed my kick.

5 . . . 4 . . . 3 . . .

But before my foot could touch it, the ball was already high in the air. I lost my balance and came down on my back. Helpless, I lay there watching as it soared over me — straight into the goal.

Time!

The stadium went wild. Even the benches seemed to be screaming. Laughing and shouting, the team lifted the scoring player on their shoulders.

The crowd was still chanting. "WigginsWigginsWig-ginsWiggins!"

But it wasn't me, Adam Wiggins, they were cheering now. It was *him*, Keith Wiggins, they were going nuts over.

Someone stepped on my leg as they carried my brother off the field.

I was practically crying when I woke up. How come? I wondered. How come even in my sleep my brother always beats me? I could understand if it were Keith's dream. That would make sense. Of course he'd be sure he was the hero in his own stupid dream. He's full of himself, my brother. He thinks the only reason there are other people on the planet is so there's someone to admire him. But this was *my* dream. It was my dream, and I still lost out to Keith. I might as well have been awake. It didn't really seem fair.

I opened my eyes slowly. Elvis, my dog, was stretched out across my legs, sound asleep, and on the other side of the room my brother was still snoring. My brother is the only person I know who sleeps flat on his back with his hands under his head. Most of the time I don't notice, but this morning it really bothered me. I looked over at him. He was lying there as if he were watching a film on the ceiling. He had a big smile on his face. With my luck, Keith was prob-ably having the same dream I'd had. I hid my head under my pillow. I really hated to see him looking so happy.

Anyway, to punish Keith for stealing my goal, I didn't wake him up like I usually did. Keith always sleeps through the alarm. My dad says that Keith could sleep through a rock concert, even if it was a heavy metal band and it was playing at the foot of his bed. I left my brother snoring away and took Elvis for his morning walk.

Elvis and I have two routes for his morning walk. If it's nice and we have time, we take the long one. The long one goes up to the end of our street, over the footbridge, and down the other side of the railroad tracks and back again. If it's raining or I'm in a hurry, we just go once around the block.

It was a nice day, and I was still upset about my dream, so Elvis and I took the long route. He stopped every three inches to sniff something, so I had plenty of time to think about Keith stealing my goal like that.

The weird thing about my dream was that I don't even play soccer. I mean, I play soccer, but not for real. I just fool around in the park after school with Midge. Midge is my best friend. His real name's Jerome, but he's not very tall so my brother started calling him the Midget and it kind of stuck. I'm not very good at soccer, but Midge is worse. My brother always gets picked first for teams, and I'm always picked fourth or fifth, but Midge is always picked last. Most of the time when we do play a game, nobody will pass Midge the ball unless they have absolutely no choice, because Midge always fumbles or falls over or passes it back to the other team. Even though the one time I ever scored was an accident, at least I managed to get the ball in the right goal.

My brother plays soccer for real. He's on a team with real uniforms and real games and real trophies. Keith's a star, if you want to know the truth. He was even trying out for this junior national team that was going to go to California and play these other junior teams from all over the country. He even had his photo in the local paper when his team won the area league championship. The caption underneath said: A FUTURE PRO? Keith's grinning like he just won the Cup Final. He had the picture on the corkboard over his desk. It made me want to puke. The only picture on my corkboard was of Elvis the time he got stuck up a tree. I taped a piece of paper to it that said: "Bird Dog."

The worst thing is, Keith isn't just good at soccer, he's good at all sports. He swims, he plays baseball, he skates, he runs, he even does gymnastics. You'd think he was in training to be a superhero or something. You know, in case Batman got a cold or something. My mom said Keith's just very physical.

"Tell me about it," I said. "I'm the one he's always beating up."

My mom said that wasn't what she meant. She meant that Keith is a natural athlete. Some people are. And some people aren't.

"You mean like me," I said.

My mom patted me on the head the same way she pats Elvis on the head. "You're good at other things," she told me. "You have your own special talents." She didn't say what they were.

So that morning Elvis and I were walking along, him sniffing and me trying to think of all the other things I was good at, when I realized we were right outside Mrs. Lim's house. I'd been so busy brooding about Keith that I'd forgotten about Mrs. Lim.

Mrs. Lim lives at the end of our street. She has this big ginger cat named Honey. Elvis hates Honey. Honey doesn't like him much either. That's why I usually make sure we walk on the opposite side of the road — only this morning I forgot.

"Uh-oh," I said to Elvis. "We better get out of here before Mrs. Lim sees us."

But it was already too late. Honey was on the windowsill. Her fur was standing up so much she looked like she'd been pumped full of air, and she was making this sound between a growl and liftoff. Elvis started barking and trying to walk on his back legs.

"Come on, Elvis," I grunted. I dug in my heels and pulled on his leash with all my strength. "Come on, boy. Let's go home. Don't you want to eat?"

But the only thing Elvis wanted to eat right then was Honey. He was trying to drag me to the window.

"Please, Elvis," I begged. "You can have toast and strawberry jelly if you'll come home now." Elvis loves toast and strawberry jelly. He was still pulling forward, but his ears went up at the mention of strawberry jelly. "Extra jelly," I promised. "Extra jelly and lots of butter."

I really think he would have let me take him home then if Honey hadn't begun to wail. It was the creepiest thing I'd ever heard. Like something out of *Poltergeist*. You know, like some deranged demon had taken over Honey's body. Elvis thought it was creepy, too, because that was when he lost it completely.

I guess it's lucky Mrs. Lim has a hedge in front of her house. If she didn't have a hedge in front of her house, there would have been nothing to stop Elvis from jumping straight from the sidewalk to the windowsill. But because Elvis had to clear the hedge first, Honey had a chance to escape. Mrs. Lim opened the front door just as Elvis yanked the leash out of my hand and hurled himself at the window. Sounding like she was being sucked into a sea of ectoplasm, Honey jumped down and shot past Mrs. Lim. Elvis ran after her.

Mrs. Lim was already screaming at me. "Do something, Adam Wiggins!" she was screaming. "Stop that dog!"

I did something. I went after Elvis. Only I didn't go along the sidewalk to the front door like I should have. I panicked. Mrs. Lim was carrying on like the Hound from Hell was after her, and Elvis and Honey were going ballistic. The three of them were making so much racket that I decided to take the shortcut—through the hedge.

Mrs. Lim's hedge came up to my chest. I figured I could jump it the way Elvis had. I jumped. It's a good thing I'm thin, or it could have been worse. I could have been the first boy in America to drown in shrubbery. I didn't clear the hedge like Elvis did; I landed in the middle.

Mrs. Lim was still screaming. "Do you hear me, Adam Wiggins? Get that monster out of my house!"

I tried to pull myself out, but my foot was jammed in some branches and there were all these other branches poking into me, making it hard to move. "I can't," I yelled back. "I'm stuck!"

Mrs. Lim was waving her hands in the air. "What's wrong with your parents, putting a little boy like you in charge of a creature like that?" Mrs. Lim screeched. "Don't they have any sense? Your brother's the one who should be walking that dog. Your brother could control him."

And then she ran back into the house to rescue her cat, and I had to get out of her stupid hedge by myself.

Chapter Two

I was afraid I was going to miss Midge. We always meet on his corner and go to school together, but this morning I was late because of what Elvis and Honey did to Mrs. Lim's kitchen. Which was more or less destroy it. She wouldn't let me go home till I helped her clean up. She said it was the least I could do. And then, when I did go home, not only did I have to listen to Keith yell at me for not waking him up, but I had to watch Keith just about choke to death with laughter over what had happened. Then my mom made me wash off Elvis and put antiseptic on my scratches from the hedge before she'd let me leave the house again. Midge was there waiting for me, though. He was looking at his watch, but he was there.

"What happened to you?" he wanted to know. "I was just about to go."

I ran up to him. "You won't believe it," I panted. "I've only been awake about an hour and I've already had one of the worst days of my life."

I told Midge what happened while we walked to school. First I told him about my dream.

"It was more like a nightmare," I told him.

Midge sympathized. "I pity you," said Midge. "It's bad enough having Keith around when you're awake. I'd hate to have him around in my sleep, too."

Then I told him about Mrs. Lim.

"You should've heard her, Midge," I said. My voice squeaked, I was that upset. Usually I'll shut up if my voice is squeaking because Keith says I sound like a girl. But today I didn't care. "She said all I do is cause trouble. *Me!*" I squeaked some more. "I get the blame as usual, and it's all Keith's fault."

It really was all Keith's fault. Elvis and Honey wouldn't hate each other if it weren't for him. Keith used to sneak Honey down to our house and hold her up outside the front window. "Elvis!" he'd call. "Elvis, there's somebody here to see you." Then Elvis would go berserk, and Keith would just about wet himself laughing. Keith only stopped doing that because one time Elvis went through the window. The vet said Elvis could have been really hurt if he hadn't been going so fast. I got the blame that time, too.

"Mrs. Lim wouldn't stop babbling about what a credit Keith is to my parents and how I should try to be more like him," I went on.

Midge understood. He knows my brother almost as well as I do. My brother torments him, too.

"It's like telling somebody to be more like Frankenstein," said Midge.

"Even after I helped her straighten up the kitchen, she was still screaming at me. She wouldn't shut up about how I'm so little and weak, and how it's too bad I don't take after Keith." I kicked a stone across the street. It stopped in the middle of the road. "Sometimes I really wish Keith had never been born. Then nobody could compare me to him all the time."

Midge stopped sympathizing. "It's only Mrs. Lim," said Midge. "Who cares what she thinks? Her cat smells like rotten cheese."

"It's not just Mrs. Lim," I argued "It's everyone."

"No, it isn't," said Midge. "It's only Mrs. Lim. And you. You're the one who's always comparing you to Keith. I think you're getting a complex about him."

I gave Midge a look. Midge has been my best friend forever, but he can be really annoying when he wants to be. And sometimes he doesn't even have to want to be — he just is.

"You mean like you've got a complex about being short?" I snapped back.

Midge pushed his glasses up his nose. "That's different, Adam. I *am* short. But just because you're not like Keith doesn't mean there's anything wrong with you." He shook his head. "Be logical, will you?" Midge is into logic. He's very smart. "It'd be pretty weird if Keith weren't bigger and stronger and couldn't play soccer better. He's thirteen and you're only nine."

I can be logical, too. "But that's not the point, is it?" I asked. I got another stone into position. This time I was aiming at this one leaf a few yards ahead of us.

Midge's eyebrows rose over the rim of his glasses. "What is the point then?"

I made my kick. I hit a tree. "The point is that for my whole life I'm always going to be Keith Wiggins's brother. No matter what I do, or where I go, I'll always have to live with that."

"So?" Midge demanded. "That's not so bad. My whole life I'm never going to be anybody's brother."

Boo-hoo. Midge isn't just an only child, he's also adopted, but I couldn't see that he had anything to complain about. Knowing you were never going to have a brother like Keith was even better than not having one.

"I'll tell you why it's so bad," I said. I jammed my hands into my pockets. "It's like always being Robin, that's why. No matter how hard I try, I'll never be Batman. I'll never get to drive the Batmobile. I'll never outsmart the Penguin. I'll always be the little guy in the green tights who says dumb things and never knows what's going on."

Midge groaned. "You're exaggerating as usual, Adam," said Midge. "I'll admit Keith's better at some things than you are, but that's no big deal. There are tons of things you're good at that Keith is lousy at."

He sounded like my mother.

"Yeah?" In spite of the fact that he sounded like my mother, hearing Midge say that made me feel a little better. My mother would say nice things to me just so my feelings wouldn't get hurt, but Midge always tells me the truth.

Midge nodded. "Yeah."

I waited to hear all the things I was good at that Keith was lousy at. Midge didn't say anything. "Like what?" I finally asked.

"Like what?" Midge pretended he was thinking really hard. He scratched his hair and puckered his forehead. "Gee . . ." he said. He sighed. "There must be something. . . ."

I gave him a shove. "Get off it," I said.

"No, really, Adam." He shoved me back. "I'm sure there must be something."

We were still laughing and shoving each other when we saw these three kids coming toward us. They were about Keith's age. We'd seen them around before. You could tell just by the way they walked down the street that they were trouble. They were laughing, too, like they'd just seen the funniest thing they'd ever seen. I knew right away that they were laughing at us. So did Midge.

"I guess it's too late to cross over, huh?" he whispered.

"I think so," I whispered back. We didn't want them to

think we were afraid of them. They were the kind of boys who would love the idea that you were afraid of them.

"Well, look who's here," said the biggest of the three. "If it isn't two of the Seven Dwarfs."

"Yeah," said the one on his right. "Sleepy and Dopey."

They came to a stop about three feet in front of us, blocking our way. The one facing me was tall and thin and his hair was cut so short it was hard to tell what color it was. The one facing Midge was tall and chubby and had almost black hair and really light blue eyes. The one in the middle was the biggest. He wasn't just tall, he was broad and solid and had a scar over his right eye. He looked like he was going to be the Terminator when he grew up. Only meaner.

Midge moved to the right and I moved to the left, but the boys on the outside moved with us. The one in the middle just smiled.

"Where do you two think you're going?" asked the boy in the middle. "You hear Snow White calling or something?" He had a lot of thick blond hair and small cold eyes. I didn't think much of his smile.

I glanced at Midge. "We're in a hurry," I said, praying I wouldn't squeak. "We have to get to school."

That made all three of them laugh.

"You have time," said Scarface. "Who's going to care if you're a few minutes late?"

"Yeah," said the chubby one. "Who's going to care?"

Scarface took a step forward. I had to force myself not to take a step back. He put on this really sweet voice. "Besides," he said, "we want you to hang out with us for a while."

"That's right," the thin one chimed in. "We want to get to know you better."

Midge made a show of looking at his watch. "Gee," said Midge, "maybe another time. It's really getting late."

Scarface acted like he hadn't said anything. "That's a nice watch," he said. He reached out his hand. "Let me see it, will you? I think it's just like the one I have."

Midge pulled his arm away.

"We really have to go," I said quickly. Midge and I were standing so close together that we kept bumping into each other. "Now."

"What's the big deal?" asked Scarface. "Just let me see the watch."

"Yeah," said the chubby boy. "Let him see the watch."

Midge held up his arm and pulled back the sleeve of his jacket. "There," he said. "That's the watch."

I could tell from Midge's voice that he was scared. This didn't surprise me, because I was scared, too. I wasn't sure what was going to happen, but I knew it probably wasn't going to be something I'd like.

Midge stepped on my foot. "Come on, Adam," he mumbled. "Let's go."

We moved forward. They didn't move back.

Boy, did I wish I could fly. My heart was pounding so hard I could hear it. My palms had started to sweat. I didn't know what to do. Keith would've known what to do.

Just then two women came out of the house beside us. All five of us turned to watch the women come down the path. One of them had a baby in a stroller. The baby was stuffing a cookie into its face, and the women were chatting away. The one who wasn't pushing the stroller opened the front gate. Midge and I looked at each other.

What Keith would've done was he would've shoved those creeps out of his way. But I wasn't Keith. I was more subtle.

"Wow," I said, practically shouting, "what a cute baby."

Midge waggled his fingers at the baby. "Hi," he said. "What's your name?"

Chewed up cookie dribbled down the baby's chin. The women smiled at us in this vague way and turned to walk past. Not looking at the other boys, Midge and I went with them.

As soon as we got to the corner, we started to run.

"I'm really glad I waited for you," Midge said as we turned into the road our school is on.

"I'm glad you waited, too," I said. The bell rang.

"What would we have done if we'd been alone?" asked Midge.

It was a good question.

Chapter Three

You'd think a day that started with your dog landing in Mrs. Lim's breakfast and continued with someone threatening your life couldn't get any worse, wouldn't you? I mean, if you'd had to scrape the jam off Elvis's ears or if you'd seen the look in those creeps' eyes, you'd sort of assume that you'd hit the bottom. *This is it,* you'd have said to yourself. *Things can only get better from now on.*

But you'd have been wrong.

The only people still in the yard when we finally got to school were pigeons.

"I don't believe this," I said to Midge. "Why is this happening to me? Now we're going to get expelled for being late." We raced through the gates.

"There you go exaggerating again," gasped Midge. Because he's short, he has to run twice as fast. "You know Mrs. Vorha. If we sit down quietly like we've been there all the time, she won't even notice."

I know I tend to exaggerate now and then. My mom says it's because I have a very active imagination. My brother says it's because I'm crazy. "If Adam were a bike, he'd only have one wheel," Keith always says. He thinks he's a riot.

I took the steps two at a time. "Maybe you're right," I said. After all, it always took a few minutes for the class to settle down. Mrs. Vorha usually spent those few minutes writing stuff on the board or pulling dead leaves off the plants on the windowsill. If we slipped in without making any noise and went straight to our seats, she probably wouldn't say anything even if she did notice. I opened the door.

It was usually pretty noisy while everyone was settling down, but today the room was silent. Or almost silent. One voice was speaking. One deep, male voice.

"I'd like to thank you two gentlemen for deciding to join us," said the voice.

I was so surprised I stopped dead. I'd forgotten we were having a substitute for a few days because Mrs. Vorha had some special conference on education to go to.

Midge had forgotten, too. He ploughed right into me. I sort of tripped into the room and landed on Rose Montoya's desk. Rose is one of these girls who always has a lot of things on her desk. Not just things you're supposed to have on your desk, like pens and paper and books, but all sorts of cute little things in pastel colors. It all went flying. Rose hit me over the head with a pink ruler with kittens on it. "You idiot!" she shrieked. "Now look what you've done. You're the one who's going to pick it all up."

Everyone who wasn't already laughing started laughing then. I could even hear Midge's giggle. Midge's giggle sounds like someone spitting out a mouthful of water. The only person who didn't think it was totally hilarious was the teacher who wasn't Mrs. Vorha. I could feel him glaring at me while I crawled around on the floor.

Finally, I found the last two things — an eraser that looked like a rabbit and a star-shaped sharpener — and got to my feet.

"If you think you've disrupted this class enough for one morning, perhaps you'd sit down now," said the substitute.

"Yes, sir." I dumped the rabbit and the star on Rose's desk and collapsed in my chair.

The substitute picked up the attendance book, his beady eyes going down the page. "And you are . . . ?" he asked.

"Adam," I mumbled. "Adam Wiggins."

"Wiggins?" He raised his head. "Adam *Wiggins?*" You'd think he'd never seen a nine-year-old boy before the way he was looking at me. "*You're* not Keith Wiggins's *brother,* are you?"

I could tell it wasn't really a question.

No, I felt like saying, *I'm his sister.*

• • •

I don't remember much of what we did in school that day, because I was too busy brooding about Keith. When I thought it over, it seemed to me that people were always saying, "*You're* Keith Wiggins's brother?" Like they couldn't believe we came from the same planet, never mind the same parents. Every time I got a new teacher, or tried out for a team, or joined a club, or went someplace where Keith was known, I always got the same reaction. Whoever it was would look at me for a few seconds and then he'd shake his head like he must have misheard me, and then he'd say, "Wiggins? You mean *you're* related to *Keith Wiggins?*"

I was still brooding when we got out of school. On Wednesdays me and Midge usually went to the park to play soccer or just fool around. This was a Wednesday so we headed to my house to get Elvis and the ball.

"I'm really tired of everybody acting so surprised when they find out I'm Keith's brother," I complained as we walked along. We were taking the long way back to Chestnut Drive. Midge and I hadn't said anything about it, but we'd both automatically gone straight out of the gates instead of turning right the way we usually did — just in case those boys were around.

"You mean like the substitute?" asked Midge.

"No," I said. "Like everyone."

"I wouldn't let Mr. Altman get to you." Midge offered me the bag of potato chips he'd saved from lunch. "He only acted like that because we were late." He bit into a chip, chewing slowly. "And because you made such a spectacle of yourself." He glanced over. "Didn't I tell you to sit down quietly? You know what substitutes are like. They have to prove they're in control right away or they might as well go home."

Personally, I wished Mr. Altman *had* gone home. "He didn't act like that because we were late," I said. "He acted like that because he thinks Keith's Superman and I'm Jimmy Olsen."

It turned out that Mr. Altman knew my brother really well. Mr. Altman had taught Keith's class for a couple of months when the real teacher was having a baby. All day long, Mr. Altman called on me every chance he got, and every time he did, he found some reason for mentioning my brother and how I was nothing like him. Keith never disrupted the class. Keith always paid attention. Keith would have known what the provinces of Canada were. Mr. Altman liked Keith almost as much as Keith liked Keith.

"You're exaggerating again," said Midge. "Mr. Altman doesn't think you're Jimmy Olsen. He thinks you're Lois Lane."

"Oh, hahaha," I said. "Maybe you should become a comedian if you ever grow up."

We turned into Chestnut Drive. Neither of us said anything, but I could tell Midge was as relieved as I was that we'd made it home without running into those creeps, because we both slowed down at the same time.

Just then Mrs. Pitelli, who lives next door to us, popped out of her front door like a cuckoo popping out of a clock. She's always doing that. My father says Mrs. Pitelli is Chestnut Drive's Early Warning System. He says having Mrs. Pitelli next door is better than an expensive burglar alarm and a whole lot cheaper. My mother says Mrs. Pitelli doesn't have much to do. Mrs. Pitelli's old and she smells like baby powder, but she's all right. She makes great brownies.

"Oh, Adam," called Mrs. Pitelli. "Adam, do you think you could do me a favor?"

Midge and I stopped in front of her gate. Mrs. Pitelli's always needing a favor. Either a lift to the supermarket, or someone to run to the candy store or change a light bulb for her, that sort of thing.

"Sure," I said. She was holding a big jar of pickles. "You want me to open that for you, Mrs. Pitelli?"

Mrs. Pitelli shook her head. "Oh, no, no," she said. "I don't think you'd be strong enough, honey. Could you ask Keith to come over when he gets home?"

It was a warm, sunny day, so the park was really crowded. There must've been about a million people playing ball and flying kites and throwing frisbees at each other. Elvis is all right with soccer balls and footballs because they're hard for him to fit in his mouth, but you have to watch him with frisbees. We hadn't been able to find my soccer ball, which meant my brother must've "borrowed" it, so we decided to walk where there weren't so many people. Neither of us felt like running around for an hour trying to get some kid's frisbee back from Elvis, if we didn't have to.

There are a lot of cool things in the woods of the park. Elvis likes to sniff around for rabbits and birds, and Midge and I like to explore. There's a stream and a couple of ponds and a lot of fallen trees you can climb over. There's even this old hollow tree that's so big you can get inside it. That afternoon we pretended the hollow tree was a starship and that we were intergalactic policemen hurtling through space on a secret mission. By the time we were ready to head for home, I was in a pretty good mood.

"Let's go out by the snack bar and get some ice cream," I suggested. I was off the trail, hunting for another stick to throw for Elvis. Elvis loves chasing sticks, but he doesn't understand that he's supposed to bring them back.

"Adam," said Midge.

"My treat."

I could sort of feel Midge come closer to me. "Adam, look over there."

I didn't turn around. "Just a second," I said. "If I can get a couple of sticks, I won't have to stop again for a while."

"*Now*, Adam." Midge kicked me.

I turned around. I looked. Three boys on mountain bikes were coming down the hill.

"So?" I said. Lots of people cycle in the park even though you're not supposed to.

"Don't you recognize them?" asked Midge.

I looked again. The boy on the green bike was thin. The boy on the pink-and-yellow bike was chubby. The boy on the black bike looked like the Terminator as a kid, or maybe just the son of the Terminator. They were pedaling even though they could have coasted.

"It's *them!*" hissed Midge, just in case I hadn't caught on yet. "The teenagers from hell."

I don't suppose it really mattered whether I recognized them or not, because it was pretty obvious from the way they were grinning and pedaling like mad that they recognized us.

"Well, look who's here!" shouted the one on the black bike. "If it isn't our little friends from this morning, Dopey and Sleepy."

"You have the time?" the one on the green bike was screaming.

The chubby one laughed. "Yeah, what time is it, Sleepy?"

Midge put his hands behind his back. He was so close to me by now that if I'd moved, he would have fallen over. "What are we going to do?" he whispered. I was glad he sounded as scared as I felt.

"Come on," said Scarface. He leaned over the handlebars, and stretched out his arm. "Let me see your watch."

I glanced around. Except for Elvis, who was sitting by my feet, wagging his tail while he waited for me to throw him a stick, there was nothing around us except trees. There wasn't a woman with a stroller in sight. No one was going to rescue us this time.

"There's only one thing we can do," I whispered back. It wasn't what my brother would have done. "Run." I figured even twenty-one-gear mountain bikes would have trouble cutting through the woods.

I'm faster than Midge, so I took the lead. I could hear Midge panting behind me, but I didn't look back. I just kept on going. Elvis passed me, barking and bouncing. He thought it was a game. Suddenly I didn't hear Midge anymore. Instead all I could hear were thick rubber tires crunching over twigs and leaves and voices screaming, "Hey, where are you going? Don't you want to hang out with us?" and a lot of unpleasant laughter. I still didn't look around. I didn't want to know how close they were. *Keith would be laughing, too, if he could see you now,* said a voice in my head. *Keith wouldn't run.* But I didn't care about Keith right then. I was so scared even my feet were sweating.

Head for the trees! I told myself. *Head for the trees!*

I headed for the trees.

The teenagers from hell headed for the trees, too. I'd been wrong about how much trouble mountain bikes would have getting through the woods. They didn't have that much trouble at all.

I'd never run so fast or so hard in my life. It felt like my heart was going to punch its way out of my chest. I might've made it, too, if it weren't for Elvis. He was so excited that he started running around me in circles.

"Get out of the way!" I gasped. "Elvis, get out of the way!"

He must have thought I was calling him or something, because instead of getting out of the way, he stopped dead. But I didn't. It was like hitting a log. I flew over Elvis and landed headfirst in a bush for the second time that day.

That cracked them up.

"Have a nice trip this fall, Dopey?" one of them cackled.

Then this hand grabbed hold of me and hauled me to my feet. It was the big one with the lousy personality. "Why were you running away from us, Adam?"

I couldn't believe it, he'd remembered Midge saying my name.

"Don't you like us?" He sounded like I'd hurt his feelings.

The thin creep flicked a twig over my head. "Yeah, Adam, why don't you like us?" he asked. "We never did anything to you."

Scarface smiled. He reached out to pick a leaf from my shoulder. "Not yet, anyway."

The three of them thought this was really hysterical.

Scarface put his hand back on my shoulder. "Have we, guys?" He was still smiling. "We haven't done anything yet."

"Nah," said the chubby creep. "We haven't done anything."

The thin one winked. "We just want to be friends."

Scarface patted my shoulder a couple of times. "Yeah, real good friends."

He's going to hit me, I thought. *He's going to hit me and I'm going to cry. For the rest of my life, every time I see this cretin he'll call me crybaby and hit me.*

I figured I might as well make another run for it. I made to pull away, but his grip tightened and he yanked me forward.

That was when Elvis went nuts.

"What happened to you two?" asked my mother.

Midge and I stopped so fast we bumped into each other. I hadn't seen my mother lurking on the stairs. I thought she was in another part of the house and we'd be able to sneak up to the bathroom and clean up before she saw us. I should be so lucky. Sometimes I think my mom has radar.

"Us?" I asked.

"Hi, Mrs. Wiggins," said Midge.

My mom smiled at Midge. "Hello, Jerome." But she didn't smile at me. "Yes, you," said my mom. "You're filthy."

"We were fooling around in the park," I said. I prayed she hadn't noticed that I was limping a little. I must have twisted my ankle when I fell over Elvis.

She came down the last few steps. She made the same sound she made the time she found the slug in her salad. "Look at you!" She was practically shouting. "Both of you are covered with scratches."

This was an exaggeration. Maybe I was sort of covered with scratches because first I'd landed in Mrs. Lim's hedge and then I'd landed in that dumb bush, but Midge wasn't. All Midge had was a couple of tiny cuts from climbing up a tree to get away from the bikes.

"It's from this morning," I said. "Remember?"

"You didn't have that many scratches this morning." My mom was staring at me so hard I almost thought she was counting them. She brought her face right up to mine. "Some of those scratches are fresh," she said. She turned to Midge. "And so are the ones on Jerome."

Just then Keith came strolling in from the kitchen. He looked at me and started to laugh. "You been walking

Elvis through Mrs. Lim's hedge again?" He really cracks himself up.

My mother gave him a look. "Stop it, Keith. This is serious. I want to know what you two have been doing to come home looking like that."

I grabbed Midge's sleeve and started edging past her. "I told you," I said. "We were fooling around in the park."

My mother shifted to the left. "Fooling around doing what?"

I shrugged. Midge shrugged. We'd agreed that we wouldn't tell my mother what had happened because she'd only get all worried and upset, but we hadn't actually agreed on what we would tell her.

Keith folded his arms across his chest. He had this really dumb grin on his face. "Yeah, Adam. Tell Mom. Fooling around doing what?"

"Just shut up, Keith," I ordered. "This is none of your business."

"Adam," said my mother. "I'm waiting."

From where she was standing, my mother couldn't see Keith without turning her head. He stuck his tongue out at me. "Yeah, Adam, Mom's waiting."

Midge smiled. I smiled. "Just fooling around."

Elvis and I stopped in the doorway to the living room. My parents were sitting on the couch, watching television, and

Keith was on the floor doing pushups. "Good night," I said.

My mom and dad looked up, but Keith just kept counting under his breath.

"Don't tell me you're going to bed already," said my mother. "It's not even nine yet."

I yawned. "I'm really tired," I said. Which was true. Running for your life can really whack you out.

"I hope you're not coming down with something," my mother said. She looked like she was thinking of taking my temperature. "You don't think any of those scratches are infected, do you?"

"I'm fine, Mom." She'd already put enough antiseptic on me to disinfect a hospital. I yawned again. "I've had a very exhausting day."

"I know," said my mother. "Fooling around."

"Baby," muttered my brother. He was in the eighties but he wasn't even out of breath.

"I am not a baby," I protested. "I'm tired, that's all."

"And so you should be," said my brother, still counting. "Destroying Mrs. Lim's kitchen must've taken every ounce of strength you've got."

If I hadn't been so tired, I would have thrown something at him.

"Stop it, Keith," said my father. "Good night, Adam."

I shut the door.

Besides being tired and hurting in about sixty different places, I wanted to go to bed early so I could be alone to think. The only time you get any privacy in my house is when you're in the bathroom or everybody believes you're asleep.

I was already thinking as I got into my pajamas. When Keith was my age, he was always getting into fights. Now he never got into fights because he was so strong nobody wanted to fight him. I turned out the light. And he was a soccer star. Nobody bullies a soccer star. I pulled down the blankets. I got into bed. I screamed.

I didn't mean to scream, but I couldn't help it. My feet had touched something warm and mushy. Something disgusting. I could smell it. This was just what I needed. First the dream. Then Mrs. Lim and Honey. Then the teenagers from hell. Then Mr. Altman. And now this. Vomit. The perfect end to a horrible day. My brother had put vomit in my bed. I was still screaming as I threw off the blankets and landed on the floor.

And then I heard it. The unmistakable sound of Keith William Wiggins pissing himself laughing.

"I'll get you for this!" I screamed. "I mean it, you android. I'll get you for this."

"You and what army?" The light went on. Keith was leaning against the door, doubled up. Tears were running down his cheeks.

I looked at my feet. There was dog food all over my toes.

"Serves you right for not waking me up this morning," said my brother. "I was nearly late for school."

I should have known he'd get even with me for that. My brother never lets me get away with anything.

Chapter Four

My dad had left for work and Keith and his best friend, Charlie Donaldson, were doing a few hundred laps in the pool before school, so my mom and I were having breakfast by ourselves.

"Mom," I said. "Mom, if you could only have had one child, which one of us would you have picked?"

She looked at me. I almost thought she was going to laugh. "What's brought this on?" she asked.

I carefully buttered my toast. "Nothing," I said. "I was just wondering, that's all."

She put down her coffee. "You were just wondering."

"Uh huh." I nodded. Our eyes met. My mom has this way of looking at you as if she can read your mind. It makes it hard to keep secrets from her. I smiled in what I hoped was an encouraging way. "You know," I said.

My mother didn't know.

"Why would you wonder a thing like that?" Her eyes narrowed and she squeezed her lips together, which isn't a good sign. It means she's thinking. "What's Keith been telling you this time?"

"Nothing, Mom." I figured she must be remembering the time Keith told me I was adopted and that if I didn't shape up, his parents, Mr. and Mrs. Wiggins, were going to give me back. "I was just wondering, that's all. I mean, what if God told you you could only have one son, which of us would you have wanted it to be?"

Her eyes narrowed even more. "He didn't tell you your father lost his job and we'd have to put one of you in a foster home again, did he?"

"No, Mom, it's nothing like that." I was really sorry I'd opened my mouth. I should have known she wouldn't tell me the truth.

"Because it's a ridiculous question," my mother was saying. "You know your father and I love both of you the same."

"But you can't," I said. This was the last thought I had had just before I finally fell asleep the night before. That not only did Keith do everything better than I did, and not only did teachers and other grownups like Keith better than they liked me, but that my parents couldn't love us equally, the way they were always saying they did. "We're completely different. You have to like one of us more than the other."

"Of course you're completely different." My mother leaned toward me. She was looking very sincere. She always looks sincere when she doesn't want to hurt my feelings. "That's why we don't have a favorite."

I wasn't sure I followed that. It seemed to me that if two things were so different you were bound to like one more than the other. You know, I like peanut butter and I like chocolate, but I like chocolate more than I like peanut butter. "But Keith's stronger than I am, and smarter than I am, and better at sports —"

My mother interrupted me. "And you have a lot of terrific qualities and abilities that Keith doesn't have."

"Like what?" I suppose I was hoping she'd say, *like a great personality,* or even, *you're a lot nicer.*

She picked up her coffee cup. "Like an overactive imagination," said my mother.

"What are you doing?" asked Midge.

I looked up. He was lifting the top of his sandwich to check that his mother hadn't snuck something into it that he didn't like. "I'm making a list," I said.

Satisfied that there was nothing in there but tuna salad and some dead lettuce, Midge took a bite. "What kind of list?"

I put down my pencil. "It's a list of all the things Keith does better than I do, and all the things I do better than Keith."

Midge chewed slowly. "I was right," he said. "You are getting a complex. Maybe you should talk to my mom." Midge's mother is a psychotherapist.

"I don't need to talk to your mother." Talking to my mother was bad enough. Midge couldn't forget to empty the trash without Mrs. Greaves coming up with at least six different reasons why he hadn't remembered.

Midge pulled his chair around the table so he was sitting beside me. "What have you got so far?"

I showed him what I had so far.

Things Keith Does Better:	*Things I Do Better:*
Baseball	Being tidy
Swimming	Making my bed
Skating	Helping around the
Soccer	house
Running	
Gymnastics	
Fighting	
Wrestling	
Science	
Math	
Making stuff	
Fixing things	
Ruining my life	

Midge sipped his juice. "There isn't much in your column," he pointed out.

Like he needed to, right? Like I didn't already know there wasn't much in my column.

"Oh, gee," I said. "Really? How come I didn't notice that?"

The trouble was that the more I'd thought about it, the more I'd realized that it wasn't just that Keith could do things that I couldn't do, it was that anything I *could* do, he did better. I figured that even if me and Keith were the same age, I'd still be smaller and weaker. Even if I were older than Keith, he'd still be good at soccer and stuff like that and I wouldn't. Even if Keith were five, he wouldn't have let Elvis drag him into Mrs. Lim's hedge. I was lucky I'd come up with as much in my column as I had. At first the only thing I could think of was that I don't have any fillings in my teeth and my brother does.

"You don't have to get an attitude," said Midge. He put down the container. "What about writing?" he suggested. "Mrs. Vorha really liked that essay you did on being someone else."

It was true, Mrs. Vorha had liked my essay. She'd liked it so much she even entered it in this contest one of the big cookie companies was running to encourage children to write creatively. We had to put ourselves in someone else's shoes. A lot of the girls pretended they were models or actresses, and most of the boys pretended they were rock stars or football players. My essay was about what it would be like if I couldn't walk and had to go around in a wheelchair. I got the idea from a documentary on TV that I watched with my dad. I made Midge pull me around in my old wagon after school every day for a week, so I could really see what it was like. It was horrible. I couldn't go into stores, or on buses, or anything. I stopped counting how many times I fell out going over a curb. Mrs. Vorha said my essay was the best in the class. She said not only was it very well written but it showed a lot of sensitivity, too.

"I don't know," I said. "I don't think Keith cares if he can write or not." Not the way I wished I could play soccer. "Do you figure it still counts?"

Midge nodded. "Sure," he said. He bit into his sandwich again. "And anyway, Adam, you have to put down something."

Normally, I can't wait for the bell to ring at the end of school, but that day I spent the last half hour of class watching the hands of the clock and wishing they wouldn't move to three-thirty so fast. I felt safe when I was at home, and I felt safe when I was in school, but I didn't feel safe in between anymore.

Midge must have been feeling the same way I was because the first thing he said as we left the classroom was, "I think we should take the long way again."

It was raining hard, so we decided to walk our bikes. It was Thursday. Thursdays we usually go to my house.

"Maybe we shouldn't've run like that yesterday," Midge said as we pushed our bikes through the school gates.

I looked over at him. He wasn't looking at me, but I could tell what he was really thinking. He was thinking, *Keith wouldn't have run. . . .*

"Oh, right." I made a face. "We should've stayed there and let them torment us."

Midge turned to me. "We could've stood up to them," he suggested. But what he was thinking was, *Keith would have stood up to them.*

I could hardly believe my ears.

"And we could have been pulverized," I pointed out. I didn't bother mentioning that he was the one who climbed the tree.

Midge shrugged. "Maybe." *Keith wouldn't have been pulverized,* he was thinking.

"*Maybe*? You mean like *maybe* the sky isn't blue?"

Midge went back to staring at the sidewalk. "It's just that now they know we're afraid of them, they won't leave us alone." *Keith wouldn't be afraid.*

I wished Midge would stop thinking about Keith. I wished I would, too.

"They already knew we were afraid of them," I reminded him. "And, anyway, they weren't going to leave us alone, Midge. They were going to take your watch."

"Yeah," mumbled Midge, "I guess they were. But my

mom says you don't solve problems by running away from them. My mom says the only way of solving a problem is to stand up to it."

We turned the corner and I caught my breath. My heart banged into my ribs. I grabbed hold of Midge's arm. "It's too bad your mother isn't here right now, then," I said.

"Ow," said Midge. "You're hurt—"

And then he saw what I saw. Down the street, facing in the direction we should have been coming from, were Scarface and his friends. Even though it was pouring, they looked really happy. You know, the way sharks look happy when they smell blood.

"They've got their bikes!" hissed Midge. The reason we'd ridden our bikes to school even though it was raining was because we figured that if we did run into the teenagers from hell, we'd at least have a chance of getting away from them. For some reason we hadn't thought they might be on their bikes, too. Midge groaned. "Now what are we going to do?"

"I thought we were going to stand up to them," I snapped back. "Isn't that what you wanted to do? Isn't that the only way to solve our problem?"

"It's too late for that now," said Midge. "Now that we've already run away from them once they have a psychological advantage."

I stared at the three boys. They were goofing around,

laughing and hitting each other while they waited for me and Midge. The smallest one was twice the size of Midge. All the chubby one would have to do was sit on us. I didn't even like to think about the one who looked like The Terminator.

"They have more than a psychological advantage," I said. "They're a lot bigger than we are, too."

I looked around, trying to decide which direction we should take. If we went back to the school, we could loop around and come out a few blocks over from where the teenage mutant thugs were waiting for us. If we went to the left, we could take the underpass and come out on the other side of the highway.

And then Midge started screaming. "Get on your bike, Adam!" he screamed. "They've seen us! They're coming! Get on your bike!"

I turned. They had seen us and they were coming.

Midge was already on his bike. "Adam!" he was shouting. "Adam, come on!"

At least it solved the problem of which way we were going. There wasn't any time to go back toward the school. We were going straight ahead, down the underpass and across the highway.

The rain was in our favor. It wasn't stopping them, but it was slowing them down a lot. If they'd been able to go faster, they would have caught up already.

Midge disappeared down the underpass. I followed.

We both screamed "Look out!" at the same time. Right ahead of us, with their backs to us, was a woman with two little kids walking beside her.

At the sound of our voices they all stopped dead. Midge hit his brakes and pulled to the right. I pulled to the right and hit Midge.

The little kids started crying and the woman started screaming at us. Which was probably the best thing that could have happened, because when I looked up, I saw that the creeps were still coming. They were laughing hysterically and coasting slowly down the ramp. They rode right behind the woman and the kids, but the woman was so busy yelling at me and Midge that she didn't even notice them.

Scarface pointed his finger at us. "You two little nerds have been asking for trouble," he said in this flat, soft voice. He winked. "And next time you're going to get it."

"You look at me when I'm talking to you," screamed the woman. "Don't you realize someone could have been hurt?"

I felt like saying that someone *had* gotten hurt — me and Midge — but I couldn't look at her. I was still watching the teenage thugs. Scarface stopped a few feet away from us and turned back. He was staring right at me. "My friends will take care of Sleepy, Adam," he grinned. "And I'll take care of you."

"You know what I wish?" Midge asked.

"That someone could beam us up now?" I answered. It was what I was wishing.

"No," said Midge. "I wish your brother were here."

If Midge weren't my best friend, I think I might have hit him.

Chapter Five

I leaned over the banister and peered into the kitchen. My brother was sitting at the table, reading a comic while he shoveled cereal into his face. My mother was standing with her back to me, putting bread in the toaster. With a little luck, I figured I could get to the front door without either of them seeing me.

My brother heard me the second my feet touched the hall. "Where are you going?" he asked in this really loud voice. He didn't even glance up from his comic.

But as soon as she heard Keith, my mother turned from the toaster with a slice of bread in her hand. "Where are you off to?" she demanded.

She was mad at me because I'd come home with my pants ripped and my bike broken. The frame must have gotten kind of bent when I ran into Midge. My mom said I was going to have to pay for it. Which meant I might be able to ride it again by the time I was twenty. My brother said if I wasn't so useless, I could fix it myself. He'd fix it himself if it were his bike.

I held up my book bag and made a face that said I

thought it was pretty weird that she should ask what I was doing. "It's Friday morning," I said. "I'm going to school."

"Hey, you're improving, Adam," said my brother through another mouthful of cornflakes. "You actually know what day it is. We'll teach you to tell time next."

"Shh, Keith," said my mom. She was staring at me hard, trying to read my mind again. "*Now?*" She waved the bread at me. "Isn't it a little early for you to be going to school?"

It *was* a little early. It was forty-three minutes early, to be exact. But Midge and I had come up with a plan for living until Saturday. The first part of the plan was avoidance. If we didn't run into those boys, they couldn't hurt us. That's why we'd decided to leave for school earlier than we usually did. If we'd had to leave for school at dawn, we would have.

I concentrated on not looking guilty and on not looking into the eyes of Caroline Wiggins, Private Investigator. "We've got some stuff to do before school starts," I said. Which was true. We had to survive.

P. I. Wiggins drew her eyebrows together. "I thought you said you were late getting home last night because you had stuff to do after school." Didn't she ever forget anything?

"I did," I said. In the end, apologizing over and over, we'd walked along with the woman and her kids till we were sure the teenage terrorists had given up. We'd gone so far out of our way that my mother called Mrs. Greaves to see if we'd gone to Midge's house instead. "But now I have more stuff to do."

"Don't lie," said Keith. "Tell Mom the truth. You and the Midget are so slow, the only way you can get to school on time is if you leave before daylight."

I ignored him. "So I'm going now," I said to my mother. "Midge is waiting for me." I started edging toward the door.

She blocked my way. "Why are you dressed like that?" she wanted to know. She forgot nothing and she questioned everything. Mrs. Vorha would have loved having my mother in her class. Mrs. Vorha is big on the inquiring mind.

I was all innocent. "Dressed like what?"

She put a hand on my shoulder. "Dressed like that." She pulled the glasses I was wearing away from my face so I had to look into her eyes. "You don't usually wear a baseball cap and sunglasses."

The second part of our plan was disguise. Midge and I figured that if we dressed differently than we usually did, those creeps wouldn't recognize us even if we did meet up with them.

The words "baseball cap" and "sunglasses" caught my brother's attention. He took one look at me and started choking with laughter. "Dig the android!" he howled. "He thinks he's in a Hollywood movie!" He dropped his comic. "What movie do you think you're in, Adam? *The Weakling Kid*?"

"Leave me alone!" I shouted back. "Everybody wears baseball caps."

"Not everybody like you," said my brother. "Losers like you still wear knit hats and parkas."

"Keith," said my mother, but she was looking at me.

"Get off!" I ordered. If my mom hadn't been holding on to my glasses, I would have gone over and kicked him.

"That just better not be *my* baseball cap," said my brother.

I stuck my tongue out at him. "Don't worry, I wouldn't want to catch something from *you*. It's the one Uncle Bill brought me back from New York."

My mother finally let go of the glasses. "Is this the new fad or something?" she asked. She sounded relieved. "Is that what this is all about?"

She was a genius. "That's it!" I was practically laughing myself. "It's the new fad, Mom. It's really cool."

"If *you're* into it, it's about as cool as molten lava," said Keith.

"That's enough from you, Keith Wiggins," snapped my mother. But she was still looking at me. "What about breakfast?" she asked. "You're not going to school on an empty stomach, are you?"

Breakfast! Here I was wondering if I was going to live

through the morning, and my mother was worried about breakfast. If I didn't hurry, the only thing I was going to be having was a knuckle sandwich. I snatched the bread from her hand. "I'll eat this on the way."

My mother shouted something about after school, but I was moving too fast to really hear what she said. I was through the door before she realized there wasn't even any butter on the bread.

It was a good thing my mother didn't see Midge that morning or she would have been worried about a lot more than my breakfast. He's been my best friend forever, but I only knew that the figure leaning against the tree was Midge because he was standing at the end of Midge's road and because he was short.

I waved, but he didn't wave back. Midge was wearing sunglasses and a baseball cap, too, but he also had on a denim jacket that was miles too big for him. The jacket and the hat both looked like they probably belonged to his dad.

"Is that you, Adam?" Midge asked as I came up to him. He lifted the glasses. He's practically blind without his prescription lenses.

"No," I said. "It's Spiderman." Up close, he looked even weirder than he had from a distance. I punched him in the arm. "You're supposed to be in disguise, Midge. Not in costume."

He punched me back. It didn't hurt, though, because the sleeves on his jacket were so long they covered his hands. "It was either this or one of my mom's hats and my old winter jacket."

If you asked me, he wouldn't have looked any weirder in something pink with roses on it. If we did run into those kids, I figured it might not be so bad — there was a pretty good chance that they'd kill themselves laughing.

I suppose the good news was that we didn't run into *them*. The bad news was that we ran into Mr. Altman instead. He was just locking up his car when Midge and I came through the gates.

Midge said, "Good morning, sir."

I said, "Good morning, sir."

Mr. Altman didn't speak at first. Instead he just stared at us in silence, his eyes going from Midge to me and back again. I wished Midge had worn his own jacket. I wished he didn't have to look over his sunglasses to see. And I really wished my Uncle Bill had brought me back one of those dark blue baseball caps that said NY in white letters, not a bright green one that had Have a Nice Day written across the front in orange thread.

At last Mr. Altman thought of something to say. "What is this?" he asked. "Halloween?"

• • •

"Stop worrying, will you?" I said. Midge was shuffling along beside me, looking at his watch. We'd given up on our disguises, so Midge had his regular glasses on now and could see. "It's Friday. They're not going to hang around for hours just to beat us up. I guarantee they're gone by now."

Midge made a disbelieving face. It's funny, but even though he's adopted, he can look exactly like his mother. "I still think we should've stayed at school a little longer."

I sighed. "Midge," I said, "if we'd stayed any longer, the janitor would've locked us in." We slowed down as we reached the corner.

"Um . . ." said Midge. He'd slowed down so much he was practically walking behind me.

We came to the corner. I looked left. The street was empty except for a lady with one of those wicker shopping carts and a couple of high school girls, laughing like someone was tickling them.

"You see?" I turned back to Midge. "I told you they wouldn't be there."

Midge was looking right. "They *couldn't* be there," he said.

I started to say that that was what I'd been trying to tell him all along, that they couldn't be there, but I didn't get any further than "That's . . ." There was something about the way he said "they couldn't be there" that made me follow his eyes. Coming toward us on the pavement were three boys on mountain bikes. They were coming like guided missiles. This time Midge didn't ask me what to do.

He was halfway up the street before I knew what was happening. There was a long line of people getting on a bus near the corner and he was heading for them.

I started to run. My brother would've caught up with Midge in about half a second, but I'd only gone a few yards when the skinny kid screeched to a stop right in front of me, cutting me off.

"Where do you think you're going?" he sneered.

I could see Midge getting on the line for the bus. He was practically standing on top of the man in front of him. Midge looked back at me. He looked the way I felt: helpless.

"I . . . uh . . . nowhere," I stammered. Which was true. Not only were he and his bike blocking the way in front of me, but the other two boys had come up behind me and were blocking my retreat.

"Well, look who's here," said the big one, acting like this was some big surprise. "Our little friend, Adam." He smiled. "We've been looking for you."

This news made the three of them laugh. It made me want to make myself invisible.

Scarface got off his bike and let it crash to the ground. He came over and put a hand on my shoulder.

"You know, you've really been bothering me a lot, Adam," he said softly. "And I don't like that."

Midge was getting closer to the door of the bus, but he was still looking back.

"Me?" I was trying really hard not to squeak, but it wasn't working. "I haven't done anything."

"Haven't you?" asked Scarface. He grabbed hold of my shirt and put his face close to mine. He smiled. "I'll tell you what you've done," he said softly. "I'm trying to be friends with you and you keep running away." He twisted my shirt. "You think you're too good to hang out with me and my friends, Adam, and I don't like that. You're hurting my feelings."

He was hurting my neck. "No, I don't," I managed to gasp.

"What?" He gave me a shake. "What did you say, Adam?"

Midge was right at the steps now, waiting to climb up.

I swallowed hard. "I . . . I . . . I said that wasn't true."

Scarface turned to his friends. "He says it isn't true that he doesn't want to hang out with us. What do you guys think?"

"He's lying," said the chubby one.

"That's right," agreed the one who was practically bald. "He's a liar."

Midge put his foot on the first step and looked back again. He looked like he was going to throw up.

Scarface yanked me even closer. "You see, Adam? It is true. Why are you lying to me?" He gave my shirt another twist. "I don't like being lied to either, Adam. I think you owe me something for all the trouble you've been causing me. Don't you?"

My heart was going crazy. I felt like I might throw up, too. "I . . . I . . ." Or faint.

"Hey, look at him!" laughed the skinny one. "He's shaking like a girl."

"What's the matter, Adam?" laughed Scarface. "Don't tell me you're scared?"

His pals started impersonating chickens.

My brother wouldn't have been scared by these creeps. My brother wouldn't have wanted to run away and cry. My brother would have slapped Scarface's hand from him and then he would have shoved him out of his way. But I wasn't my brother. I was so scared I couldn't even speak.

All of a sudden, Scarface let me go. I nearly fell over. Then he reached into my pocket and came out with a handful of coins.

Midge was at the top of the steps. The only thing I wanted right then was to be standing behind him. Or maybe in front of him.

"Is this it?" Scarface was staring at the coins he was holding. It was half my allowance for the week. "*Is this all you have?*"

It wasn't all I had. I had my life's savings, nearly thirty dollars, in my book bag because I didn't like to leave it at home in case my brother decided to "borrow" some. He was always doing stuff like that.

I nodded.

He held out his palm so the other two could see how much was there. "Well, it's not enough," he said quietly. "You're going to have to do better than that."

In my heart I knew Mrs. Greaves was right. It's better to stand up to things than to run away from them. Running away doesn't solve anything. Only Mrs. Greaves wasn't with me right then. And Midge was handing the driver his fare.

The teenage thugs were still figuring out how much money they had and how much more they wanted. For at least a few seconds they'd forgotten about me. Midge looked around again. If he could have beamed me up, he would have. The driver was waving him into the back of the bus. I still had a chance to get away. It wasn't a big one, but it was a chance.

I took a deep breath, and then I ran. I just plowed straight through the three of them.

"You little creep!" screamed Scarface. I could hear him picking up his bike. "Just wait'll I get my hands on you!"

Don't look back, I told myself. *Run, run, run . . .*

"You'll never get away from me, Adam," Scarface was

shouting behind me. "You hear me? Never! I'll find out where you live. I'll wait outside your school. . . ."

Run, run, run . . .

The front tire of Scarface's bike touched my back. I hurled myself through the doors of the bus just as they were about to close.

"I was afraid you weren't going to make it," said Midge as I collapsed into the seat beside him in the back. "I didn't want to leave you, Adam, but I didn't know what to do."

"It's all right. I didn't know what to do either," I panted. "Boy, that was close."

Midge was looking out the rear window. "It's still close," he informed me. "They're right behind us. They're following the bus."

I didn't want to see them. I kept my eyes straight ahead. "Ignore them," I told him. "Don't let them see you looking at them. They've got to give up eventually."

Midge leaned back in his seat. "What if they don't?" he asked quietly. "What if they don't give up?"

This wasn't something I really wanted to think about. My brother never gave up. He might have to wait days to get even with me for something, but it didn't matter. He'd wait years if he had to. Sometimes he had to wait so long that neither of us could remember what it was he was getting even for. What if these creeps were like Keith?

"Then I guess we'll have to live on this bus for the rest of our lives," I said. "It's a good thing it goes by your mother's office, at least she'll be able to throw some sandwiches in the window every day."

"It's not funny," said Midge. "What happens the next time they catch us?"

I closed my eyes. I could still hear Scarface screaming, *You'll never get away from me, Adam. Never!*

Unless one of us turned into Captain America all of a sudden, the next time they caught us we were going to be hurt.

Chapter Six

My mother was standing in the doorway as I came up the path. She started shouting the second she saw me. "Adam Wiggins!" she was shouting. "Where have you been? I had to send your brother out looking for you."

"What'd you do that for?" I shouted back. That was all I needed. Like I didn't have enough problems. Now Keith would never let me forget that my mother made him go look for me like I was a lost dog or something. He and Charlie would kill themselves laughing over that one.

"I'll tell you what I did it for," yelled my mother. "I did it because I was worried. It's nearly six o'clock."

What with all the stress I was under and having to walk home from miles away because we couldn't get a bus back, I was pretty exhausted, but I acted cool and regular, like it wasn't any big deal. "You didn't need to worry," I said. "It's Friday." I strolled past her. "I was with Midge."

My mom was right behind me. "But you weren't supposed to be with Midge, Adam. You were supposed to be with Dr. Morris. I couldn't believe it when his office called to see why you never turned up."

I stopped in the middle of the hallway. I turned around. "Dr. Morris?" Dr. Morris is my dentist.

She folded her arms in front of her. She sighed. My mother has this way of sighing that's more like a scream. She says my brother and I are the only ones who can make her sigh like that.

"What did I tell you when you were rushing out of here this morning?" she demanded. "Didn't I remind you about your appointment?"

So that was what she'd shouted after me. I couldn't decide whether she'd be madder if she knew I hadn't heard her or if she thought that I had. "I guess I forgot," I said at last.

"You forgot." It wasn't a question, but it wasn't exactly a statement either. It was more like she was taking notes. "You've been acting very strange the last few days," said my mother. "You come and go at odd times, you come home covered in scratches or with your pants torn and your bike broken—"

"I told you," I said. "It was an accident. Me and Midge crashed in the rain."

"I know what you told me," my mother answered. "But I'd still like to know what's going on."

I couldn't tell her the truth. I know my mother pretty well. If I told her these bigger boys were bullying me and I was afraid of them, she'd make a big stink about it. She'd find out who they were. She'd go up to the school and talk to their teachers and the principal, and then she'd talk to their parents. She's like that, my mom. She'd probably make me go with her to the school. She'd make the teenage terrorists apologize to me in front of everybody. She'd make them promise never to bother me or Midge again. Just the thought of it made me want to crawl into a hole. Not only would I be totally humiliated in front of the whole world, but it wouldn't make any difference. They wouldn't stop bothering me and Midge after that. They'd bother us more. They'd hound us. They'd torture us. They'd use us for tissues. But even worse, once the whole world knew what chickens me and Midge were, other kids would start bullying us. We'd never get away from them unless we moved to France. Or maybe Venezuela.

"Nothing's going on," I said. I crossed my fingers and looked my mother in her X-ray eyes. "Nothing at all."

"You're sure?" asked my mother. "You wouldn't lie to me?"

"Yes, I'm sure," I said. I wouldn't lie, but I would stretch the truth.

"So where were you and the Midget?" asked Keith.

He was sitting on his bed, getting undressed, but I was already under the covers. I didn't want to tell Keith where I'd been any more than I wanted to tell my mother. Unless he died laughing, which, of course, was possible, he'd torment me with it for the rest of my life. He'd start calling me the Chicken the way he called Midge the Midget. Pretty soon everybody would be calling me Chick the way everybody except grownups called Midge Midge. My life would be ruined. I pretended to be asleep.

Keith threw his socks at me. They smelled like a backed-up sewer.

I sat up, choking. "What are you trying to do, kill me?" I screamed.

My brother started laughing. "I knew you were awake," he said. "You can't fool me."

"I don't want to fool you." I hurled the socks back at him, but instead of landing in his face, they landed in the middle of the floor. "I want you to leave me alone."

This time he threw one of his sneakers at me. It bounced off the wall and just missed Elvis. Elvis yelped and jumped off the bed.

"Is that the thanks I get?" asked Keith. "Charlie and me gave up a game to go looking for you and the Midget, you ungrateful little cretin. The least you can do is tell me where you were."

"I wasn't anywhere." I turned my back on him. "Me and Midge went to the park."

"Without the mutt?"

Most of the time it's hard to imagine how anyone as nice

as my mom could have given birth to Keith. I mean, my mother's a regular human being, but my brother's more like something that crawled out of a cave. A dark underground cave, filled with bats and dinosaur bones. Every once in a while, though, he reminds me of my mom. Like right then. Keith would have made nearly as good a detective as Caroline Wiggins.

"We didn't have time to come back and get him," I said. "We were in a hurry."

"Don't lie. We checked the park. You weren't there."

"You couldn't check the whole park," I answered. "You must've missed us."

I heard the springs of his bed creak, and then the next thing I knew Keith was sitting on top of me.

"Get off!" I screamed. He weighs about a ton.

My brother pushed a pillow over my head. "Tell me," he ordered. "Tell me where you were. What dumb thing are you and the Midget up to this time?"

"We're not up to anything," I mumbled. It's hard to breathe and talk at the same time when someone's sitting on you and you're being suffocated. I tried to throw him off but I couldn't move. "I told you, we went to the park."

"I mean it, turd breath," said Keith. He started bouncing up and down on me. "You tell me or you're going to be sorry."

Boy, did I wish I were an only child. At least Midge only got bullied when he left the house. Me, I didn't even have to leave home. I didn't even have to leave my room.

"I am telling you," I grunted. "We went to the park."

My brother pulled the pillow off and threw it on the ground. Then he just sat there, looking into my eyes. "You're telling me that you're coming home late all the time and leaving early and coming back with your bike smashed up and there's nothing going on? That's what you're telling me?"

I stared back into his eyes. I could see my reflection in them. I looked real small. And for about a nanosecond and a half I wanted to tell Keith the truth. He was my big brother. He wasn't afraid of anybody or anything. I wanted to ask him what I should do. I didn't like the fact that those boys knew my name. It made me feel like I really never would get away from them. That no matter what I did, they'd be able to find me. I wanted to ask Keith what he'd do if someone was bullying him. I had this incredible urge to beg Keith to help me.

He pressed down so hard on my stomach I thought I was going to gag. "You better tell me the truth if you know what's good for you," said my brother.

The urge to beg him to help me passed. I remembered the time I told Keith I was afraid of spiders, and he put a pregnant spider in my shoe. When I went to put it on, there were about a billion baby spiders crawling all over it. I nearly died. And then there was the time I told Keith I hated cauliflower so much that I only pretended to eat it, and he told my mother. She nearly killed me. I knew what was good for me. Keeping out of my brother's way was good for me.

"I am telling you the truth," I answered. "Nothing's going on."

Keith gave me one last long hard look and then he let me go. "You better not be lying to me," he said. "Or you'll be sorry."

At least some good was coming out of this. Normally a threat like that from my brother would have worried me, but not now. I was too afraid of the teenagers from hell to be afraid of Keith, too.

Chapter Seven

I didn't get a lot of sleep Friday night. I was in my own bed with my brother snoring on the other side of the room and Elvis snoring at my feet, but whenever I closed my eyes, I saw those boys. They were standing around me in a circle, smiling at me the way Lex Luthor smiled when Superman lost his powers. They were getting ready to beat me up and take all my money. I tried to make myself think of something else, but they wouldn't go away. I buried my head in my pillow, but I could hear Scarface laughing and saying, "What did I tell you, Adam? You'll never get away from me, Adam. Not ever."

It was true. I never would get away. I lay awake for hours, tossing and turning, thinking about how I would never get away. At first those boys had been hassling us just because we were there, but it was personal now. They really wanted to get us. The big one really wanted to get *me*. They knew where we went to school, because it was the only elementary school in that neighborhood. They knew my name. And they'd threatened to find out where I lived. There was no way I'd be able to escape them. Every day, for the rest of my life, they'd be waiting for me. They'd push me around. They'd steal my things. They'd humiliate me over and over again. Unless I stopped them.

I stared up at the ceiling. There was a shadow on it that looked like a fist. How was I going to stop them? If I could stop them, none of this would ever have started.

I stared at the wall, thinking about what I *could* do. I could tell my mother. That was out. I could tell my brother. That was out. I could run away from home, but that was out, too. I mean, I couldn't run very far when my mother wouldn't let me go any farther than the school in one direction and the park in the other, could I?

I put my head under the pillow again. There was only one other thing I could do. I could stand up to them. I tried to picture myself standing up to them, but all I saw was Scarface knocking me down.

I came out from under the pillow and started staring at the ceiling again. *You could stand up to them,* I told myself. *Standing up to them isn't that hard. You just have to do it.* I went back under the pillow. The hard part would be standing up to them and staying alive.

Until we figured out a way that we could stand up to the teenagers from hell without being creamed, Midge and I decided to lay low.

We spent Saturday at his house, playing on his Nintendo. We played most of the morning and all afternoon, but neither of us could beat my brother's record. Every hour or so, Midge's father would poke his head in the room and ask us if we weren't going to go outside. You'd think it was the first sunny day we'd ever had the way he carried on.

"It's a beautiful day," he kept saying. "Why don't you boys go out and get some fresh air? You don't want to spend the weekend cooped up in a room."

We told him that we did want to spend the weekend cooped up in a room, but we didn't tell him that we wanted to spend the weekend cooped up in a room because we knew that if we went out, we'd run into those bullies. I'd rather have spent the rest of my life in a room than be beaten up. We just said that we were having a good time.

Midge's father said that when he was a boy, he was outdoors playing ball or riding his bike no matter what the weather was like. When he was a boy, he couldn't stand to be indoors. He craved physical activity and adventure.

"Not us," I said with more emotion than I'd intended. "Physical activity and adventure are the last things we want."

Midge's father shook his head sadly. He said he knew they should never have let Midge's grandparents buy him Nintendo. He said he knew it would destroy Jerome's creativity and make him indolent. I didn't know what indolent meant, but I knew better than to ask. Once Midge's father got started explaining something, it was hard to get him to stop. He went on for over two hours one time because we made the mistake of asking him some simple little question about whales.

Midge and I spent Sunday at my house, playing on my Nintendo. My mother was out, but my father was home. We played from the minute Keith left to meet Charlie till it was time for Midge to go home, but neither of us even came close to beating my brother's record. Whenever he remembered we were there, my father would stick his head in the room and ask us if we were planning to spend the whole day glued to "that" game. We said that we were.

"What about Elvis?" he wanted to know. "Elvis looks forward to spending Sunday outdoors."

I patted Elvis's head. He didn't wake up, but he flicked his ear. "Elvis is tired," I told him. "He wants to take it easy this weekend."

"Elvis takes it easy all week long," said my father. "He could use a little exercise." He looked from Elvis to me and Midge. "And so could you two." He shook his head. "You're certainly nothing like your brother," said my dad. "We can never keep him inside."

"Why would you want to?" I asked.

• • •

Monday morning we got a lift to school with Midge's mother because it was raining so hard that she felt sorry for us. After school, we walked home with a bunch of kids and went straight to Midge's.

"You see," I said as I followed Midge into his house. "Everything's working out all right after all."

In spite of everything, I was in a pretty good mood. Mrs. Vorha was finally back from her conference. She said it was very interesting. It didn't sound very interesting; it sounded like a bunch of teachers sitting around talking about teaching, but Mrs. Vorha said she'd learned a lot. She said the other teachers had been impressed with what we were doing in our class. I was really glad to see Mrs. Vorha, and besides that, I was really glad that Midge and I had made it safely through another day.

Midge, however, wasn't in as good a mood as I was.

He hung up his jacket in the hall. "Everything is not working out all right after all," said Midge. His eyes darted toward the living-room door. We could hear his mother talking on the telephone inside.

"Yes it is. We just have to take things one day at a time." I hung my jacket beside Midge's.

"I don't want to take things one day at a time," Midge informed me. "I can't take much more of this, Adam. I'm tired of sneaking around like a criminal."

"Don't think of us as criminals," I said. "Think of us as

spies." Spies sounded a lot more romantic than criminals. But not to Midge.

"I don't want to think of us as anything but little boys," said Midge. We could hear his mom saying good-bye. He lowered his voice. "And I'd like to see us live to be big boys." He lowered his voice even more. "I mean it, Adam, I'm tired of living in fear."

"And I'm not?" I was the one who'd had half a week's allowance stolen. I was the one whose front wheel was bent. I was the one Scarface wanted to break in two. "I'm the one who lies awake half the night, trying to come up with ways of surviving," I told Midge's back as he lead the way down the hall.

"Well you don't have to," said Midge. He shut the kitchen door behind us. "I know how we can solve this problem in about ten minutes."

"Oh, yeah?" I said. "And what's that? Call up Clark Kent and ask him if Superman could help us?"

"No," said Midge. "Tell Keith."

"Tell Keith?" I was sure I couldn't have heard him right. I was sure I must have water in my ears from walking home in the rain. But I was wrong.

"It would solve everything."

"Tell Keith?" He really thought this was a solution?

He shoved me out of the way and opened the fridge. "Yes," said Midge. "Tell Keith. What's so hard about that?"

"You want me to tell Keith that we're being bullied?"

Midge put a container of juice on the counter. "Yes, Adam. That's what I want you to do."

"And do you know what he'll do if I tell him that?" I stepped back as Midge heaved himself up on the counter so he could reach the cabinet. "Huh, Midge? Do you know what he'll do?"

Midge handed me two glasses. "Keith will take care of those kids for us, that's what he'll do, Adam." He handed me the cookie jar. "He'll make them leave us alone."

"No, he won't," I said. "He'll laugh himself sick, that's what he'll do. He'll think it's the funniest thing he's ever heard. He'll torment me with it for the rest of my life."

Midge squished up his mouth. "If I had a big brother, I'd tell him."

"If you had a big brother, he wouldn't be Keith," I pointed out. "There'll be an ice rink in hell before I tell Keith. There'll be Martians in the White House."

"Our folks'll be visiting us both in the hospital if you don't tell him," said Midge.

"That's not true." I watched Midge pour two glasses of juice. "I don't need Keith's help. I can fight my own battles."

Midge gave me a look. It was not a look of total confidence. "No, you can't," he assured me. "If you try to take on those kids, they'll knock you out cold before you even make a fist."

I picked up my drink. "Thanks for having so much faith in me," I said sourly.

"Faith has nothing to do with it," said Midge. "I'm just being realistic. We can't spend the rest of the year trying to stay out of their way. It's not only stupid, it's impossible." He bit into a sandwich cookie. "And we can't hide in our rooms every weekend, Adam. Our parents are going to force us out sooner or later."

I helped myself to a cookie. "I know that," I said. "I'm not planning to hide from them forever, Midge. I've decided that your mother's right. I'm going to stand up to them."

"Oh, sure you are," shrieked Midge. Soggy cookie crumbs sprayed all over the counter. "What are you going to stand on, Adam, an armored tank?"

"Oh, hahaha," I said. "Very funny." I took another cookie. "For your information, what I'm going to do is I'm going to learn karate."

Friday night wasn't the only night I hadn't gotten much sleep. I hadn't gotten much sleep on Saturday or Sunday night either. I kept racking my brain, trying to think of some way I could stand up to those boys and live. Regular fighting was out because they were all bigger and heavier than I was. Even if I could fight — which I couldn't — I wouldn't stand a chance. In movies people were always having duels and shootouts and things like

that, but I couldn't remember anyone ever having a duel in my neighborhood. And then, long after my parents had gone to bed on Sunday night, it hit me. The perfect thing. Karate! I'd seen it in a film. There was this skinny little kid who moved to a new city and these big boys with bad attitudes started picking on him. No matter where he went or what he did, they'd show up and they'd beat him. He was afraid to leave the house. Just like me and Midge. He got a black eye and I got cuts and bruises. His bike got messed up and so did mine. And then he met this old guy from one of those Eastern countries where they know all about self-defense, and the old guy offered to teach the skinny kid karate. The old guy made him catch flies with chopsticks and stand on the prow of a rowboat and stuff like that, but in the end the kid became this big karate expert, beat those bullies, and won the championship and all.

I figured if it worked for him, it could work for me.

Midge didn't.

"This isn't going to work, Adam," Midge whispered. He was whispering because we were in the library near our school. "Life isn't like the movies, you know. You can't change just like that."

The reason we were in the library was because I needed a book. The only person I knew who came from an Eastern country was Mrs. Lim. Even if she was speaking to me, which she still wasn't, I was pretty sure she didn't know much about karate. Gardening was more Mrs. Lim's thing. I wasn't discouraged, though. I figured I could pick up the basics from a book, and then I could practice on Midge.

"Yes, you can change," I whispered back. I pointed to the shelf of books in front of us: *Teach Yourself Tennis, Weightlifting at Home, Learn to Ski in a Weekend* . . . The number of things you could learn from books was endless. I wondered if they had one on being a human being that I could get for Keith.

"This is it." I pulled a thin black book from the shelf and read the title out to Midge, "*Karate: Its Theory and Practice.*"

He looked over my shoulder while I started flipping through the pages. There was a long introduction by the author, who was a famous martial arts expert. He didn't come from Okinawa, though. His name was Alan Draper and he came from New Jersey. There was a chapter on the history of karate and there was one on what you were supposed to wear. Then there was Course I, the Beginners Course. That was for me. It had exercises to get your mind ready. It had exercises to get your body ready. It had step-by-step illustrations of men in short jackets and loose pants flipping around other men in short jackets and loose pants. It had diagrams that showed you where to stand, and how to step, and how to move your body. It even had photographs. I grinned at Midge. It didn't look hard at all.

Chapter Eight

I walked home slowly from the library, looking at the pictures in the karate book on the way. I was so excited that for the first time in days I didn't worry about running into the teenagers from hell, I just strolled along like a normal person who isn't expecting to turn a corner and get beaten up. I imagined that I'd already mastered the lessons in the manual. I could see myself dressed in that white jacket and those baggy pants, punching and kicking and shouting out like the guys in the pictures.

I kicked open our front gate. "Uh!" I yelled. I punched the air.

"Have a good day at school, Adam?"

My mom was behind the hedge, scraping paint off some old table she got in a junk shop. She scared me, suddenly talking like that when I thought I was alone, but I managed not to scream.

I was glad I'd already put the manual in my book bag, so I didn't have to explain that. I smiled so she wouldn't think I was acting weird or anything. "It was all right."

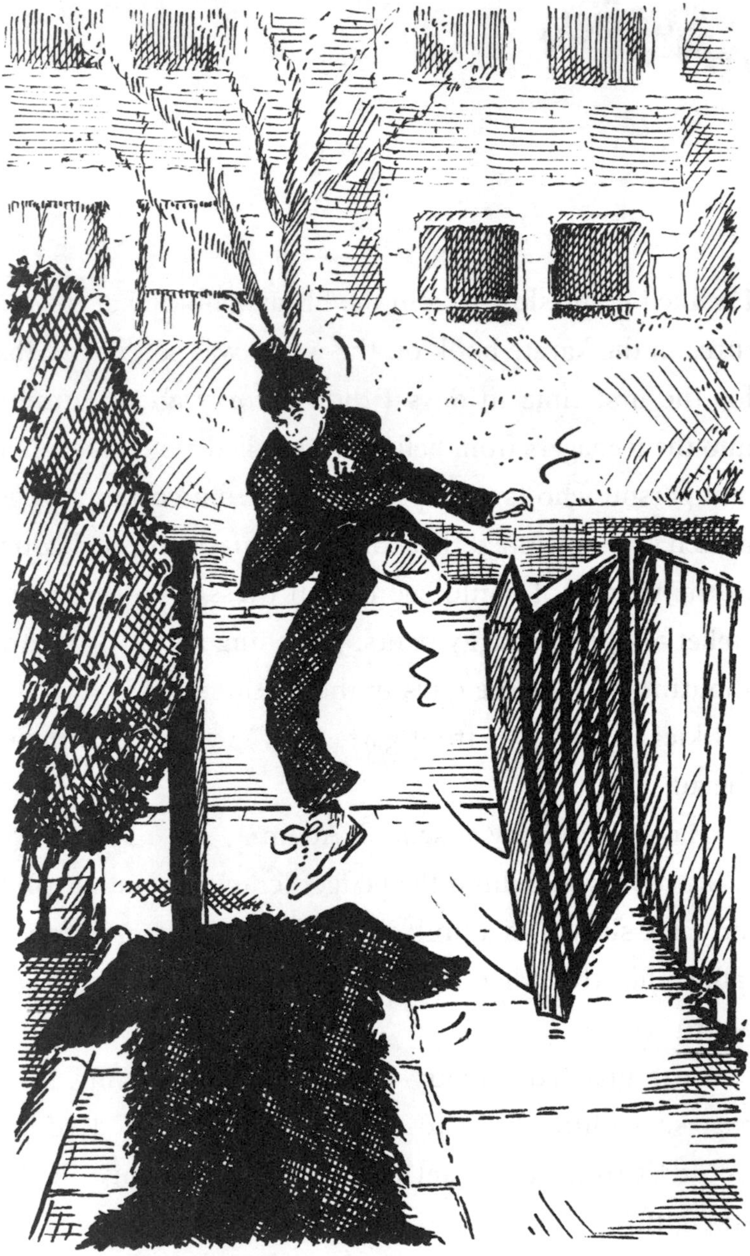

She was giving me one of her Chief Inspector Caroline Wiggins looks. "What did you do today, then?" she asked.

"Do?" I knew we must have done something, but my head was so full of *Karate: Its Theory and Practice* that at first I couldn't remember what.

"Yes," said my mother. "What did you do?"

It came back to me. "Oh, I know! Mrs. Vorha says the essay I wrote on being in a wheelchair is still in the contest. She says they'll be announcing the winner soon."

My mother stopped looking like she thought I was one of her suspects. "Why, Adam, that's wonderful! Wait till your father hears!"

I hadn't thought much about the contest when Mrs. Vorha told me about it at the end of class because I was trying to figure out the safest route to the library, but now that I saw my mom's reaction, I was feeling pretty pleased.

My mom dusted paint flakes from her hands and came over and gave me a big hug. "I must say, your father and I certainly have a lot to be proud of," she said. "Keith was chosen for the junior state team today and your essay's been entered in a contest."

"Keith was chosen for the junior team? The one that's going to play all over the country?"

"Isn't that terrific?"

My mom was still smiling, but I wasn't. Somehow,

getting my essay in some dumb cookie contest didn't seem like much next to making the junior state team.

There was some *really* good news, though. Keith was spending the night at Charlie's. I couldn't believe I could be that lucky. The only time I ever had our room to myself was when Keith spent the night at Charlie's. And the only time I could do anything private was when I had our room to myself. I couldn't cut my toenails when Keith was around without him making a major deal out of it, forget anything else. So I took it as a sign—a good sign.

I called Midge to tell him. "You see," I said. "I knew I was doing the right thing. My luck is changing at last."

"It couldn't get much worse," said Midge.

Right after supper, I told my parents I had a lot of homework to do, then Elvis and I went to my room. I locked the door. I didn't lock the door because I was afraid someone would just walk in and want to know what I was doing, but because I *could* lock the door. The one time I locked the door when Keith was around and bothering me, he unscrewed the whole knob and my dad got mad at *me*. I took the karate book out from under my mattress, where I'd hidden it, and I stretched out on my bed.

The first thing I read was the karate oath. It was something like the Boy Scout pledge. It was pretty cool. *I have no weapons*, it said. *But should I be forced to defend myself,*

my principles or my honor, then here are my weapons—
"karate"—my empty hands.

I went on to the introduction. Alan Draper and I had a
lot in common. Alan Draper decided to learn martial arts
when he was thirteen and some kids at school kept beating him up. I liked him right away. He said he tried sev-
eral sorts of self-defense, but that he liked karate best. I
hadn't realized how many forms of self-defense there were,
or how hard most of their names were to pronounce. Elvis
was snoring by the time I got through the list. Alan Draper
claimed that the coordination karate developed in you
would make it possible for three opponents to receive a
blow at the very same moment. That sounded like exactly
what I wanted. I couldn't wait to see the faces of the
teenage terrorists when they each received a blow from me
at exactly the same moment.

Alan Draper went on to talk about how much enjoyment
karate had given him in the years he'd been studying it.
There was a picture of him and he looked pretty old, so I
figured he'd been studying it for a long time. This worried
me a little. I didn't want to spend years learning karate. I
didn't have years. I'd been lucky over the weekend, but
those boys could turn up again at any time. I had to master karate in one or two days.

The next section told a little about the history and phi-
losophy of karate. I thought the idea was to be able to beat

up somebody else even if he was bigger than you were, but the book said that the spirit of karate was passive, not aggressive. It said karate was about form and balance. It said karate wasn't about violence, but about nonviolence. This was news to me. The teenagers from hell weren't interested in form and balance, and they definitely liked violence a lot. I skipped some of that section and went to the first picture where someone was flicking someone else through the air.

The one thing I'd been right about was that size didn't matter. You didn't have to be tall and built like an armored tank. You didn't have to have muscles or be able to run like a panther. You didn't have to be Captain America or Keith Wiggins to master karate; you could be *me* and master it just as well. All you had to know was when to pull back and when to push forward, where to grab your opponent and how to slip out of his way. The manual said that the beauty of karate was that it was as simple and natural as breathing, and just as effective.

And then I must have fallen asleep.

Midge and I were walking home from school. It was winter and the sky was gray. Instead of our usual route, we were walking through this big deserted field. The only things in the field besides us were these gigantic black birds, strutting around and stretching their wings. All of a sudden it started getting really dark. Midge and I didn't say anything to each other, but we both knew that something was going to happen. Something bad. We walked faster. The field disappeared. We were on a narrow, dirty street lined with old, empty buildings with broken windows and crumbling walls. There was trash all over the ground. Things were creaking and banging in the wind. Someone started laughing. It wasn't a pleasant sound. When the laughing got softer, we heard something else. We heard someone crying for help.

Midge turned to me, a look of fear and horror on his face. I put my finger to my lips. I knew that he'd recognized that voice, too. It was my brother, Keith.

I motioned Midge to stay where he was and I crept silently to the end of the street. Standing flat against a wall, I peered around the corner. Three boys were standing in a circle in the middle of the street. One of the boys was tall and thin and his hair was so short you couldn't tell what color it was. One of the boys was tall and chubby and had almost black hair and really light blue eyes. The one who was laughing was the biggest. He wasn't just tall, he was broad and solid. He looked like he was going to be Arnold Schwarzenegger when he grew up. Only really mean. In the middle of the circle was Keith. He was down on the ground and he was begging for mercy. The thin boy and the chubby boy were kicking him.

"Don't hurt him too much," ordered the boy who was laughing. "Save something for me." Then he laughed even more.

I stepped out of the shadows. "No," I said. "Save something for me."

The three of them turned in my direction.

"Adam!" gasped Keith. "Adam, get away from here. Save yourself!"

"Yeah, Adam," said the laugher. "Run away like a chicken. Go home and cry to your mommy."

Very, very slowly, I started walking toward them. "I'm not going anywhere," I said. "And the one who's going to be crying isn't me, it's you."

This made them all crack up.

The two who were kicking Keith stopped. "You!" they jeered. "What are you going to do, bore us to tears?"

I was almost up to them by then. They were facing me in a line.

Keith was sobbing. "Adam," he begged me. "Adam, please, forget about me. Just tell Mom I love her and save yourself."

"You're my brother," I said. "I'm not leaving here without you."

The big boy spat on the ground. "You don't scare us," he said. "You're nothing but a weakling. You don't have any muscles. You can't swim or play soccer. You run like a girl. You can't even control your dog."

I smiled, slowly. "There's one other thing about me you should know."

"Oh, yeah?" The three of them sneered. "And what's that?"

This time I laughed. "I have a triple black belt in karate."

I was still laughing when the last one crumbled to the ground. I tied them up with some rope that was lying around. They were crying like babies and kicking the pavement. I helped Keith to his feet.

"How can I ever thank you?" he whispered. His voice was choked with emotion. "You saved my life."

The kicking got louder.

"You don't have to thank me," I said. "It was nothing. It wasn't a big deal."

"But you're a hero," said my brother. "You're going to get a medal. You're going to have your picture in the paper."

All of a sudden Elvis and my mother were beside us. Elvis was licking my face. My mom was shouting. "Adam! Adam, you're so brave and strong! No wonder I always liked you better than Keith."

I opened my eyes. Elvis really was licking my face. And my mother really was shouting. Only she wasn't telling me how brave and strong I was and how she always liked me better than my brother. She was trying to get in.

"Adam Wiggins," she was shouting. "Adam Wiggins, you open this door!"

Chapter Nine

I thought I'd be able to start kicking and punching right away, but Alan Draper had a whole bunch of things he said I had to do first. Like prepare my mind. I wasn't sure what he meant by that so I sat with my eyes closed for a few minutes, trying to think about nothing, while Midge read through the manual. The next thing I was supposed to do was practice breathing, but I figured I could skip that because I'd been breathing for nine years already and knew how to do it. At last I got to the more exciting part, preparing my body. According to Alan Draper, you didn't have to be big and muscular, but you did have to be in shape.

I lay on my stomach on the floor of my room. My mother was next door fixing Mrs. Pitelli's electric blender and my brother was at soccer practice, so Midge and I had the house to ourselves for a little while.

"*Finger* pushups?" I asked. "Are you sure that's what it says? *Finger* pushups?"

"That's what it says," said Midge. He held up the book so I could see the picture. The figure at the top of the page was definitely pushing himself up by his fingertips.

"How many times do I have to do that?"

Midge frowned at the page. "Fifteen."

I got my fingertips into position, but I couldn't lift my body even a little. "What comes after that?" I asked.

"Pushups on your first two knuckles," said Midge.

"Get out of here!"

Midge waved the book at me. "It's true, Adam. After finger pushups, comes knuckle pushups."

I didn't think any better of pushing myself up by my knuckles than by my fingertips. And I figured I had about as much chance of being able to do it, too. Which was no chance at all. "What's after that?"

Midge squinted at the tiny print. "Pushaways."

That didn't sound too difficult. Living with my brother, I was used to being pushed away. "What do I do?"

Midge read out what I had to do. "Face the wall, and make your body straight from head to heels."

I stood up and faced the wall. I made my body as straight as I could.

"Your weight should be on your hands and feet," read Midge.

"Right," I answered. This was easy.

Midge looked from the page to me. "No, Adam. Your hands should be at eye level and your feet half a yard from the wall."

I corrected myself. "Go on."

He cleared his throat. "Okay," said Midge. "Now, keeping your body and arms straight, push yourself away from the wall until your weight is on your fingertips."

I pushed. I lost my balance and fell backward.

"Let's forget about all that stuff at the beginning," I said. After all, I wasn't going to beat those kids by dazzling them with my finger pushups. I was going to beat them by knocking them down with one fatal kick. "Let's go straight to the very first escape defense," I said. "It's called Resisting a Left-Hand Grab from the Front." The skinny kid was always grabbing me by my jacket, so this was perfect.

"Why can't I be the one who's escaping?" asked Midge. "How come I have to be the bad guy?"

"Because I'm the one who's learning karate," I explained for about the fourth time that afternoon. "You're just my partner."

I put Keith's swimming trophy on the manual to hold the page open.

"But I don't want to be your partner," said Midge. "I still think the whole thing's a dumb idea. I still think we should tell your brother."

I decided to do to Midge what my mother does to me when I try to argue her out of something. I ignored him.

"All right," I said. "Now here's what you do. You grab my shirt with your left hand."

Midge looked at me doubtfully. "And then what happens?"

I looked down at the book. "Then I step back on my left foot and grab your hand with my left hand while I hit your elbow with my right arm." I decided to skip the part that said, "CAUTION: This can cause a sprain or fracture."

Midge was still looking distrustful. "That's it?"

I read on. "Unless that doesn't work. Then I have to use the five-finger thrust to the eyes."

"I don't like the sound of that," said Midge. He stood on his toes and peered over my shoulder. "What's that?" he squeaked. "It says, 'TO BE USED ONLY IN AN EXTREME EMERGENCY.'"

I shoved him away. "Don't get yourself all worked up. I'm not really going to hit you. Alan Draper says to always stop before you make contact. It's just to teach my body what to do."

"What if you hit me by accident? What if you poke out my eyes?"

"Through your glasses?" He can be really picky when he wants. "I'm not going to hit you, all right? We're just going through the motions." I stood in front of him like the man in the manual was standing in front of his partner. "Now grab my shirt with your left hand."

"You swear you're not going to touch me?"

"Midge!"

He grabbed my shirt. I stepped back on my left foot. I grabbed his left hand. The bedroom door opened. I was so surprised that instead of going through the motions of whacking Midge's elbow with my right arm, I punched him in the chest. This time we both fell over.

My brother and Charlie were laughing before we hit the floor. When I looked up, they were both bent over, gasping for air. There were tears in their eyes.

"What are you two dweebs doing?" gasped Charlie. "Learning to dance?"

My brother recovered first. He'd spotted his trophy holding open the karate manual. "What're you doing with *my* trophy?" he demanded. He went over and snatched it and the book from the bed. For a couple of seconds he just stood there, looking at the manual, and then he started laughing again. "Hey, dig this, Charlie," he howled. "The munchkins are teaching themselves karate."

I pulled myself off Midge. "You leave that alone," I shouted, grabbing the book away from him. "It's mine."

He shook the trophy in front of my face. "And this is mine," he shouted back. "If you don't keep your hands off my things, you're going to need karate."

"What makes you think we don't need it now?" mumbled Midge.

I couldn't believe he'd said that. If I'd been a little closer to him, I would've kicked him for real.

Fortunately my brother didn't hear him. He was too busy laughing again. "Jeez, Adam," he was saying, "the only way that book's going to help you defend yourself is if you throw it at someone."

"Nah," Charlie hooted. "Even then it wouldn't help him. He'd be sure to miss."

Alan Draper said that if you practiced the basic strikes every day, you'd make rapid progress. The only time I could practice the basic strikes was when I was in the bathroom. Which meant that I had to take a bath at least once a day — a long bath.

I practiced while the tub was running. I practiced some more while the water got cold. I put in some more hot water and practiced while that was running. I took a really quick bath, got out of the tub as quietly as I could, got into my pajamas, and practiced a while longer.

After only one night, though, my brother was getting suspicious.

Keith was lying on his bed, reading a comic book, when I came into the room in my pajamas and robe. He watched me put my jeans over my chair and my shirt on the back of the closet. Then he threw an apple core at me.

"What's going on?" he wanted to know. "Why were you in the bathroom so long?"

I sat down at my desk to finish my homework, my back to Keith. "I don't know what you're talking about," I said.

My brother explained. "You go to school early, you come home late, and now you spend half the night in the bathroom. If I didn't know you better, I'd think you must have a crush on someone."

This was so far from the truth that I laughed with relief. "Only you could come up with something so dumb."

"It takes one to know one," said Keith. I could hear him throw the comic book on the floor and sit up. "So what's really going on, Adam? Why are you going miles out of your way if it isn't so you can walk by some girl's house?"

I stared at my notebook. I didn't like the way the conversation was going. It almost sounded like Keith knew something I didn't know he knew. I made my voice casual. "What makes you think we walk miles out of our way?"

"Because you and the Midget were over on Mansfield yesterday afternoon."

I couldn't help it, I looked around. "How do you know that?" I blurted out.

Keith smiled, pleased with himself. "Me and Charlie were coming back from the bike shop and we saw the two of you turning out of Mansfield." Actually, it wasn't a smile, it was a sneer. "What were you doing, Adam? Unless you've changed schools, Mansfield's at least half a mile out of your way."

I turned back to my notebook, hoping he couldn't hear the way my heart was pounding. "We were taking a walk, that's all. It's a free country, isn't it? We can take a walk if we want."

"Sure you can," said Keith. There was this long silence while I stared at my homework and Keith stared at the back of my head. "And is that why you're teaching yourself karate?" he finally asked. "Because it's a free country? Or is it just because you like falling over and making a fool of yourself?"

"I'm just helping Midge learn," I mumbled. "You know, 'cause he's so small."

"Sure you are," said Keith. "And that's why you just spent an hour in the bathroom, right? Because of Midge."

Usually I only think of good answers to my brother afterward. You know, after he's asleep or the next day or something. But this time one came to me right then. "No," I said. "I spent an hour in the bathroom because I don't want to stink like you do."

My brother doesn't have the same problem. He always knows what to say. "Don't worry about it. You stink just like yourself." A peanut shell hit the back of my head and landed on the desk.

I kept staring at the page of math I'd copied out, but all I saw was just a bunch of numbers. They didn't make any sense.

And then all of a sudden Keith said, "You're not in some kind of trouble, are you, Adam?"

I was so surprised I almost said "Yes." Instead I said nothing. I started adding up the numbers in problem number one.

Keith came over and stood behind me. "Well?" he asked. "Are you?"

"Of course I'm not." I hunched over my homework. "What kind of trouble would I be in?"

"I don't know," said Keith. "But I'm going to find out."

"There's nothing to find out," I said quickly. "There's nothing wrong."

Keith reached over my shoulder and took the pencil from my hand. "It's thirty-four, not twenty-four," he said. "You forgot to carry the one."

Chapter Ten

My brother flicked a soggy cornflake at me. "How come you're not rushing off to school?" he asked. "Don't you and Midge have something important to do this morning?"

My mom didn't say anything, but she stopped sipping her coffee and looked at me.

I would have kicked Keith under the table but I couldn't reach him and I was afraid of hitting my mom instead. It always makes her mad. Keith had been on me all night long about what Midge and I were up to. Then after we turned out the lights, he started teasing me about learning karate. He said that me and Midge learning karate was like Elvis trying to learn how to use a computer. He even made up this song about it. The only line I could remember from it was: "Watch out for Adam, though he may be small, you never can tell just where he'll fall." I tried to suffocate him with my pillow, but he threw me off and I knocked the golden retriever lamp my grandpa made us off the dresser. My mom must've been in the hall, because she was at our door as soon as it hit the floor. That's why I didn't want to make my mom mad. She already was mad. And that's why

I wasn't leaving early for school. I was hoping he'd give up if I acted like everything was normal.

"I don't feel like going early today," I said. I scooped up my cereal so hard that milk went all over.

But my brother never gives up. He smiled. "Did you show Mom that book you got?" He looked at my mother. "Adam and the Midget are teaching themselves karate," he informed her. "They're going to be the first kids in the neighborhood to earn their pink belts."

"Leave your brother alone, Keith," ordered my mother. "Me?"

"Yes *you*," said my mother, but she was still looking at me. My brother never gives up and my mother always likes to know what's going on. "Does this mean you're going to be home to take Elvis for his walk at the old time this afternoon?" she wanted to know.

"Of course I am," I answered. "Where else would I be?"

"That's what Mom and I would like to know," said Keith. "Where else would you be?"

I hadn't had a chance to tell Midge that I was going to be late, so I figured he'd have gone on without me. Only he didn't. He'd waited at the end of his road for a while like he always did, but when I didn't show up, he started to come to my house for me. He didn't want to go to school on his own. So I was surprised to get down to the end of my road and see Midge there. I was even more surprised to get down to the end of my road and see the teenagers from hell there, too.

None of them saw me, they were too busy.

The teenagers from hell had Midge up against a brick wall. The fat one and the one who was practically bald were running around, taunting Midge and laughing. Son of the Terminator was holding out his hands while Midge dug into his pockets.

I didn't know what to do.

I mean, I knew what I should do. I should rescue Midge. But even though I'd been studying karate for a couple of days, I wasn't so sure I could take on all three of them. Not at such short notice. My mind hadn't been exercised. I wished I had Elvis with me. He never bit anyone, he just barked a lot, but they didn't know that. They were scared of him.

"I think he's going to cry," the skinny one was shouting. "Look, I think the dwarf's going to cry."

The one taking Midge's money laughed. "No, he's not. He's going to wet himself."

I thought about Elvis for a second. Noise. Alan Draper said that it helped throw your opponent off guard if you shouted. He said it was like a bear growling. Or a dog barking, I figured. It gave you a psychological advantage.

The karate shout was the one thing I knew I was really good at. I decided to give it a try. Maybe if I surprised them and made enough noise, I could scare them. My house wasn't that far away. All I had to do was scare them long enough for us to get there.

I took a deep breath. And then I started running toward them, yelling and screaming as loud as I could. I didn't even look at Midge or stop or anything, I just ran right through them, howling like a dog, and then I turned back sharply, racing for my house. Everybody ran after me. I prayed that the kid right behind me was Midge and not somebody else. I ran up the path to the front door.

"Open the door!" Midge shouted. "Open the door!"

I fished in my pocket for my key. Coins and gum wrappers and stuff like that fell out.

"Hurry up," panted Midge, coming up behind me.

"Don't think this is the end of it!" Son of the Terminator was shouting. "You think you're clever, Dopey, but you owe me. You and I are going to fight."

I finally got my key in the lock and Midge and I sort of fell into the hall. My brother was just getting his jacket out of the closet. I slammed the door behind me before he could see who was outside.

Keith didn't say anything, he just stood there looking at us.

"I forgot something," I said, charging up the stairs. "Didn't I, Midge?"

Midge hurried after me. "Yeah," he gasped. "He forgot something."

"He'd forget his brains if he had any," said my brother.

After attendance, Mrs. Vorha said she had an announcement to make. "This concerns Adam," she added.

Everybody looked at me. Usually when everybody looks at me, I get embarrassed. But today I didn't care. There was a pretty good chance that I was going to be dead soon, what did it matter?

Mrs. Vorha was looking at me, too. She was smiling. "I have some very good news," she said.

The only good news she could give me was that she was leaving for Alpha Centuri in an hour and wanted me to go with her.

"Adam," Mrs. Vorha was saying, "I'm very happy to be able to tell you that your essay has been chosen as the best of its age group by the judges of the contest." I'd never seen her smile like that before. "You won, Adam! Isn't that wonderful?"

Everybody clapped.

"Adam," said Mrs. Vorha, "I thought you'd be pleased. You're going to be given a special certificate, and the local paper is going to reprint your essay. Your words will be in print. The first publication of many, I hope."

"I am pleased," I said. I forced myself to smile. "I'm really pleased." And I was. I liked writing, and I'd really enjoyed writing that essay. But all I could think was that I'd be even more pleased if I was still around to see my words in print.

They were waiting for us right outside the gates. When they saw me and Midge, the three of them carried on like we were their long-lost friends or something. They were smiling and laughing. In loud voices they said how good it was to see us and how they'd been afraid we weren't coming and how much they were looking forward to hanging out with us.

Midge grabbed my arm and tried to make me stop. "Let's go back inside," he whispered. "Mrs. Vorha's probably still around. Let's tell her what's going on."

It wasn't like I was kidding myself about what was going to happen. I stood a chance if the teenage mutant thugs grabbed me from the front with one hand, grabbed me from the front with two hands, grabbed me from the back with one hand, or grabbed me from my right side. That was as far as I'd gotten in Alan Draper's book. Anything else, though, and I was in deep trouble.

But I'd been thinking about this afternoon all day long and I knew what I had to do. I'd been scared when I charged at those boys that morning, and I'd been scared when they chased us back to the house, but afterward I'd felt better in a weird way. At least I'd done something.

I figured that one way or another they were going to beat me up, but I'd feel a lot better about it if they beat me up because I was standing up to them and not because I was running away.

"You can go back if you want to," I said, pulling free of his hand. "But I'm going with them."

Midge hesitated for maybe half a second. "Then I'm going with you," he said.

The mean one lead the way.

The fat one started walking next to Midge.

The skinny one put an arm around my shoulder. "Adam," he said, "wait'll you see the spot we've picked out. You're going to love it."

I didn't love it. It was in the park, in this little clearing in the woods.

"No one will bother us here," said Scarface. He laughed. "We'll be able to have a nice, sensible talk in private."

The skinny one patted my head. "We're going to tell you two little geeks what you're going to do for us from now on." He was patting my head really hard. "Just so's we understand each other."

"Get your hand off me," I said. I figured that if we were going to fight, I might as well start standing up to them now.

"Oooh," said the chubby kid. "Adam's got an attitude."

The skinny kid put his face real close to mine.

"Who's going to make me?" he asked. "You?"

The other two goons considered this a major joke.

I stood up as tall as I could. They didn't notice, but I didn't care. Alan Draper said the basis of karate was confidence. If you were confident and thoughtful, if you didn't give in to fear and panic, you could overcome any opponent.

"Yes," I said. "I'm going to make you."

They found this even funnier.

"Gee," said the mean one. "I'm really scared."

He reached out and grabbed me by my jacket. It was a right-hand lapel grab from the front. I wasn't sure about the right hand. Did that mean I stepped back on my right foot? The other thing was, he was holding me a lot tighter than Midge did when we practiced. He was sort of choking me.

"I'm warning you," I said. "Let go of me, or you'll be sorry."

This was my funniest joke yet.

"I mean it," I said. It was weird, but my voice wasn't shaking or anything. And I didn't feel like crying, either. I felt angry. I knew that in a few minutes what I was going to be feeling was pain and probably blood, too, but right then all I felt was mad. "I'm not afraid of you," I went on. Because I sounded so calm I figured he couldn't tell that I was lying. "If you know what's good for you, you'll let go."

"Ooooh," he squealed. "I'm really scared now."

The other two were practically wetting themselves.

"You should be scared," said a voice behind me. The teenage thugs stared over my head. "You heard my brother," said the voice. "Let go of him or you're going to be really sorry."

It was like someone had spoken the magic words or something. The mutant thug let go so fast I nearly fell.

"Wiggins," said Son of the Terminator. He was smiling, but it wasn't the way he smiled at me. He was scared. "Wiggins, is this your brother?"

Midge and I turned around. Keith and Charlie had dropped their bikes and were coming toward us. They were walking slowly, like they had all the time in the world. They looked really big. Bigger than the teenagers from hell. Talk about confidence. I wondered if Keith had ever read Alan Draper's book.

"Yeah," said Keith. "That's my brother." He looked at me. "You all right, Adam?"

I nodded. "Yeah," I said. "I'm fine."

Keith turned back to the mutant thugs. "That's good," he said. "Because anybody stupid enough to hurt my brother would have to deal with me."

It was like being in a film.

The three teenagers from hell took a step backward for every step my brother and Charlie took forward.

"We didn't know he was your brother," said the fat kid. "You know we wouldn't hurt your brother."

"Oh, sure," said Keith. "I know that." He stopped beside me. "Are these creeps the reason your bike got broken, Adam?" he asked. "Is this why you've been acting so weird?"

I nodded again, but I couldn't quite speak. Half of me wanted to tell Keith to go away, that me and Midge could take care of ourselves. But the other half of me was really glad to see him. I don't think I'd ever been gladder to see anyone in my life. It was like having Superman as your brother.

"They mugged us," Midge blurted out. "And they've been waiting for us after school and chasing us all over."

"Tough guys," said Keith. "Beating up on little kids."

"I told you," said the biggest one. "We didn't know he was your brother. We wouldn't have gone near him if we knew he was your brother."

Keith put his hand on my shoulder. "Why don't you and Midge take your bike and go home?" asked Keith. "Me and Charlie want to have a little talk with your friends."

"My bike? But my bike's broken." I looked back to where he and Charlie had left their bikes. It was true. Keith had been riding my bike, not his.

"I fixed it," said Keith. So that was why he stayed over at Charlie's the other night. That was why he'd been coming from the bike shop Wednesday afternoon when he saw us on Mansfield. "I figured if I didn't fix yours, you might borrow mine."

"So what'd you do?" I asked Keith when he finally got home. "Did you beat them up?

"No," said Keith. "I'm not going to risk hurting myself fighting with those jerks. Bullies make me sick. They think they're tough because they push around kids who are smaller than they are, but they're about as tough as cream cheese. Me and Charlie just talked to them, that's all." He sat down beside me on my bed. "You weren't really going to fight them, were you, Adam?" He was looking at me in this strange way. Like he hadn't ever really seen me before.

"I didn't have much choice," I answered honestly. "It was more like they were going to fight me."

"But weren't you afraid?"

"Not really," I said coolly. The funny thing was, once I said it, I realized it was kind of true. Standing up to those boys hadn't been half as terrifying as imagining standing up to them had been. When I'd been talking back to them, being scared hadn't mattered. I knew they would beat me up, but I also knew I wasn't going to make it easy for them.

"I'd've been afraid," said my brother. "I would've fought them, too, but I still would've been afraid."

The way he said "I would've fought them, too" made it

sound like we were the same kind of person. I stared at him. "Go on. You're not afraid of anything."

"Sure I am," said Keith. "Everybody's afraid of something. Even Indiana Jones is afraid of snakes."

It was true. Indiana Jones was afraid of snakes. I'd forgotten about that.

"And anyway," I said. "It wasn't like I was totally unprepared." I pulled Alan Draper's book out from under my pillow. "I have been reading this, you know."

Keith took the manual from my hand. "I was thinking of learning karate myself," he said slowly. "Maybe we could ask Dad if he'd let us have lessons. Then we could practice together."

"But you'll be better at it than I am," I said. I hadn't meant to say that. I'd meant to say that I thought that was a great idea, but somehow it slipped out.

Keith grinned. "Of course I will be," he said. "That goes without saying."